Praise for Kate Hoffmann's The Mighty Quinns

"[Kate Hoffmann] continues to do a wonderful job with her beloved Quinn family saga. A perfectly paced page-turner, this setup novel for the New Zealand Quinns is firmly in place and off to a great start."
—*RT Book Reviews* on *The Mighty Quinns: Malcolm*

"A winning combination of exciting adventure and romance... This is a sweet and sexy read that kept me entertained from start to finish."
—*Harlequin Junkie* on *The Mighty Quinns: Malcolm*

"Hoffmann always does a great job creating different stories for the members of the Quinn clan... This is another fun tale that organically connects to the ongoing saga of this clan."
—*RT Book Reviews* on *The Mighty Quinns: Rogan*

"This is a fast read that is hard to tear the eyes from. Once I picked it up I couldn't put it down."
—*Fresh Fiction* on *The Mighty Quinns: Dermot*

"Keep your fan handy! It was impossible for me to put this steamy, sexy book down until the last page was turned."
—*Fresh Fiction* on *The Mighty Quinns: Jack*

Dear Reader,

As most of you know, I've been writing about the Quinns for quite some time now. My first Quinn book was published in 2001. Since then, I've explored many different branches of the family, but in this new trilogy that starts with *The Mighty Quinns: Eli*, I've had to hunt down three Quinn heirs that don't even know they're Quinns.

This tangled family tree is now kept on genealogy software, which helps me sort out all the relationships and keeps track of important dates. And though the family keeps getting bigger, I find that there's always a handsome Quinn hero waiting on the horizon for me to snatch him up and give him a story.

I hope you enjoy my newest tale, featuring Eli Montgomery, the lost brother of my New Zealand Quinns—Malcolm, Rogan, Ryan and Dana. Stay tuned for two more books in this trilogy, coming up in the next year.

Happy Reading,

Kate Hoffmann

Kate Hoffmann

—

The Mighty Quinns: Eli

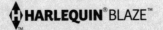

Recycling programs
for this product may
not exist in your area.

ISBN-13: 978-0-373-79844-5

The Mighty Quinns: Eli

Copyright © 2015 by Peggy A. Hoffmann

Printed in U.S.A.

Kate Hoffmann celebrated her 20th anniversary as a Harlequin author in August 2013. She has published over eighty books, novellas and short stories for Harlequin Temptation and Harlequin Blaze. She spent time as a music teacher, a retail assistant and an advertising exec before she settled into a career as a full-time writer. Her other interests include genealogy, musical theater and vegan cooking. She lives in southeastern Wisconsin with her two cats, Winnie and Gracie.

Books by Kate Hoffmann

HARLEQUIN BLAZE

The Mighty Quinns Series

The Mighty Quinns: Danny
The Mighty Quinns: Kellan
The Mighty Quinns: Dermot
The Mighty Quinns: Kieran
The Mighty Quinns: Cameron
The Mighty Quinns: Ronan
The Mighty Quinns: Logan
The Mighty Quinns: Jack
The Mighty Quinns: Rourke
The Mighty Quinns: Dex
The Mighty Quinns: Malcolm
The Mighty Quinns: Rogan
The Mighty Quinns: Ryan

To get the inside scoop on Harlequin Blaze and its talented writers, be sure to check out blazeauthors.com.

All backlist available in ebook format.

Visit the Author Profile page at Harlequin.com for more titles.

To my ever patient and always brilliant editor,
Adrienne Macintosh, who always has great ideas
when I seem to be running low.

Prologue

ANNALISE MONTGOMERY KNELT down beside her six-year-old son and combed her fingers through his mussed hair.

"Can we go home, Mama? I don't like this place."

"How did you get dirty already?" she said. Annalise glanced around the park, spying the children's equipment at the far end.

"It's just dirt," Eli said. "No big deal."

Annalise laughed softly. "But this meeting is a big deal for Mommy. I want you to be on your best behavior. No running around like some wild animal. This has to go well, all right? Agreed?"

"Yes, Mama."

He gazed up and watched as Annalise smoothed her hands over her skirt. He couldn't ever remember seeing his mom in a dress, especially not one so fluffy and shiny. She looked like a princess, and Eli was proud to stand beside her and hold her hand.

He'd held her hand during the plane ride, which had seemed to go on and on, for more hours than he could count. There was a movie and three different meals. He hadn't been allowed to get up and run around and he got yelled at six times for kicking the seat in front of him.

He'd thought flying in a plane would be exciting and cool, but it had been really boring. And now, he'd have to do it all over again when they flew home to Colorado. He wanted to go home, though. It was summer there and if he wasn't with his mom, he'd be sleeping over at his grandma's cabin on the mountain.

It was his favorite way to spend the summer, and though he enjoyed traveling on an airplane, he was sure that Nanna Trudie missed him. The minute he got home, he'd pack his stuff and hike up the mountain.

"There," Annalise said. "I want you to look at that man. See him?"

He followed the direction of her hand and noticed a tall man with dark hair and tanned skin. He had a nice smile and very white teeth, and he seemed fun. Eli could tell he liked children because he had two boys with him. The man walked over to the swings and put the boys on them.

"Who is that?" Eli asked.

"He's a very famous mountain climber. His name is Maxwell Quinn and he's climbed lots of very high, very dangerous mountains. I want you to remember that man."

"Does he go mountain climbing with you?" Eli asked.

"Sometimes," she said with a smile. "Come on, let's go meet him."

She took his hand and crossed the distance between them. The man, Maxwell, looked up and saw them coming, but for some reason that Eli couldn't understand, he sent his two little boys away to play on the slide.

Eli watched the boys and didn't care to listen to the conversation between Maxwell and his mother. It sounded like they were very angry with each other. Eli wanted to ask if he could leave, but rather than interrupt, he just quietly walked away.

The two boys eyed Eli warily as he approached them, but Eli was used to making new friends. "Hi," he said.

"Hi," the boys said in tandem.

"I'm Eli."

"I'm Rogan," one of them said. "And that's my twin brother, Ryan."

They spoke with a strange accent to their words, much like Maxwell. It made it difficult to understand them, but not impossible. They'd just invited him to play on the merry-go-round with them when Eli heard his mother call him. He glanced in her direction and saw her motioning to him. Eli gave the boys an apologetic smile and shrugged. "I guess I gotta go," he said. "'Bye."

When he reached his mother, she took his hand in hers and pulled him quickly toward the car she'd rented. "Why are we leaving?" Eli asked.

"We don't belong here," she murmured. "We need to go home."

He looked back at the boys and gave them a wave. It must be nice to have brothers, Eli thought to himself.

But that wasn't for him. He was an only child, and always would be.

1

ELI MONTGOMERY DROPPED his pack on the floor next to the door then stretched his arms above his head, working the kinks out of his neck and shoulders. He'd been traveling for nearly three days and his body and mind were completely exhausted. Now that he was home, all he wanted was a hot shower and a comfortable bed.

"Home" had been a lot of different places over his childhood and adult years. But right now, the closest thing he had to it was a small apartment he kept over his mother's outdoor outfitting store in Stone Creek, Colorado.

Annalise Montgomery owned a bungalow in town, but she'd bought that just a few years ago, long after he'd needed to reside under his mother's roof. His apartment was rent-free, large enough to store all his outdoor equipment and a permanent address for the occasional paycheck he collected. What more could a guy want?

"May I help you find something?" A pretty young salesclerk approached him with a bright smile pasted on her face. She was new.

"I'm fine," he said. "Is Annalise working today?"

"I'm afraid she's not here right now. Is there something I can help you with?"

"Nope," Eli said. "Do you know where she is?"

"That's really none of your business," the girl said.

He peered down at her name tag. "Vanessa?" Eli held out his hand. "I'm Eli. Annalise's son."

A tiny gasp slipped from her lips and her cheeks turned scarlet. "Oh, dear. I'm so sorry. I—I should have recognized you. She has a picture of you on her desk. You're very…handsome. Even with the beard."

Eli ran his fingers through his shoulder-length hair and smiled apologetically. He hadn't shaved in two months and his last haircut had been months ago.

"I'll just give her a call," Vanessa said. "And let her know you're here. She's over at The Gorge."

"The Gorge?"

"The new ski resort that Mr. Baskill is building."

"What's she doing over there? Still protesting?"

Vanessa bit her bottom lip. "Not anymore. Actually, she and Mr. Baskill have been…"

"Been?"

"I guess you could say they've been…hooking up?"

Eli frowned. His mother's behavior rarely surprised him, but this did. Last he'd spoken to his mother, she'd been spending every minute of her free time protesting against Baskill and his land-grabbing plan to build a new ski resort near Stone Creek.

Eli cleared his throat. "My mother is hooking up with Richard Baskill?" She'd called the guy a dangerous mix of Darth Vader and Donald Trump. And now, just a few weeks later, she was sleeping with him?

"I'm going to go give her a call," Vanessa said. "I'm sure she'll want to come right over." She hurried off, then quickly returned to him. "Can I get you something to drink? We have a very nice organic elderberry tea. Or you can try a sample of the new E-66 sport drink that your mother is endorsing. Although, now that I think about it, it's supposed to replace estrogen in postmenopausal women so maybe not."

"I'm fine for now," Eli said. "I'm just going to pick out something to wear from the rack here and then I'm headed upstairs to grab a shower and shave." She gave him a blank look. "I live in the apartment upstairs."

"Oh, that's you?" She winced. "We've been storing some stock up there, so forgive the mess. I'll make sure to get it cleaned up tomorrow." She sent him another nervous smile. "Just leave the tags from the clothes on the counter."

He and his mother had never had a very traditional relationship. She'd raised him on her own, and Eli hadn't known who his father was until he was fifteen. Even then, he'd never been able to talk to the man. Maxwell Quinn, a noted mountain climber and adventure guide, had died on Everest when Eli was eight. But it hardly mattered. To Eli, he was nothing more than a name on the back of a faded photo.

After Eli's birth, Annalise had stayed home for a few years, attempting to accept a traditional role as the mother of a toddler. But the moment he was toilet trained, Annalise continued her adventuring, leaving

Eli in the care of his grandmother, Trudie Montgomery, or his grandfather, Buck Garrison.

His grandparents' lives were just as nontraditional as his mother's. Buck had never married Trudie, and after the brief affair that produced Eli's mother, they each took up with an odd assortment of lovers. His grandparents tried to give him a normal life—high school, sports, hearty meals and a lot of time spent outdoors.

Eli knew at an early age that his family was different. Trudie had disregarded societal norms and raised her daughter on her own, working any odd job she could find to put food on the table. Annalise had left home at sixteen, dropping out of school to take off with a climber she'd met at a local roadhouse. A few years later, Trudie wandered into the wilderness of the Rockies, built a rustic cabin on the edge of a mountain meadow and never returned to civilization.

She spent the rest of her life writing books about feminist empowerment and a woman's connection to the natural world, turning herself and her little mountain home into a symbol for independent women throughout the world.

Most of the people around town, however, thought Trudie and Annalise were a bit crazy. There were times when Eli had to agree, although he preferred to think of them both as *unconventional*. After all, they were family—his only family—and he'd learned to accept them for who they were: two very confident, powerful women who didn't need a man in their lives to be happy or fulfilled.

Trudie had passed away seven years ago after a valiant battle with breast cancer. After a brief stint in the hospital, she'd returned to her cabin to die. Annalise and Eli had buried her in the meadow, in a coffin Trudie had built herself. After her death, her cabin became a destination for hikers trekking into the Arapaho National Forest and a pilgrimage for women who had admired Trudie's tenacity and her talent as a writer.

When Eli was home, he often spent time at the cabin, making sure the roof was still sound and the cupboards were stocked in case someone wanted to stay there, or it was needed as an emergency shelter by a lost or injured hiker. Though many other empty cabins had fallen prey to squatters or vandals, Trudie's cabin, like her memory, had been revered by those who visited, and left untouched.

"Annalise is on her way," Vanessa called from the far end of the store.

"Thanks," Eli replied.

He found a pair of cotton cargo pants and a T-shirt on the sale rack. His mother's shop was a popular stop for tourists, but she still went on climbing expeditions all over the world and led treks for breast cancer survivors, in honor of her mother's battle for both equality and survival.

Annalise had also founded one of the country's most successful breast cancer charities. She still served as the face of the group, though she'd never been interested in the day-to-day business workings.

Eli walked to the back of the store, then past his mother's office to a narrow stairway. When he got upstairs, he wove a path through the boxes that littered the hallway, stripping off his travel-worn clothes along the way.

He found a pair of scissors in the kitchen, then made his way to the bathroom. Eli stared at his reflection in the mirror for a long moment. This was the first time he'd been home without an exit strategy already planned. Usually, his visits had an expiration date, a day when he was required to leave so he could make his next adventure. Over the past few years, he'd trekked the Andes, worked a fishing boat in Alaska, hopped a freighter for Taiwan, taught a series of workshops for Outward Bound and helped film a documentary about surfing in Hawaii.

Maybe it was time to reassess his choices in life, Eli mused. Though he'd never wanted a traditional career, he felt as if he ought to be contributing in a more profound way. Both his grandmother and his mother had carved out legacies for themselves. What would his legacy be?

Some guys built powerful careers, and their lives were all about money and accumulating wealth. Others, like politicians, preferred to build their power. Others married and found their legacies in their children. And then there were those that set themselves apart by accomplishing impossible things, like climbing the highest mountain or finding a cure for a fatal disease or pitching a no-hitter.

When would he figure out his place in the world? And when would he be perfectly happy with his life? These questions always seemed to plague him at the end of one of his adventures, when he was left with just the memories and nothing more. Usually he was able to push them to the back of his mind by finding another adventure, but this time, he had nowhere to go and nothing to take his mind off of his murky future.

Eli carefully clipped off the beard, but left his hair a little long. He'd make a quick visit to the barber tomorrow. Rubbing his face, he turned on the shower and when the water was nice and warm, stepped beneath the spray and sighed.

He hadn't had a real shower, or bath, in almost two months. The luxury of hot, fresh water was almost more than he could bear and he groaned softly as he let the spray pound his back.

By the time he'd scrubbed his skin and lathered his hair, he was starting to feel almost human. The lather dripped off his body and gathered around his feet as he rinsed, then he reached for the faucet and shut off the shower. Wiping the water from his face, he yanked the curtain back and reached for a towel. He wrapped the soft fabric around his waist and strode into the bedroom to grab the T-shirt and pants.

"Look at you!"

His mother was perched on the edge of his bed, her legs crossed in front of her, her wavy gray-streaked hair falling around her face.

"Jesus, Annalise!" He clutched the towel and made sure it was tightly knotted.

"Oh, please. I've seen you naked before. Many times."

"Get out," he said, nodding toward the bedroom door.

She jumped off the bed, then threw her arms around his neck. "You're home!" She gave him a kiss on the cheek, then rubbed it in as she'd done when he was a child. "So it will last," she murmured, as she always did.

He waited for her to close the bedroom door behind her, then cursed softly. Was it any wonder that he'd never figured out the female mind? Maybe if he'd had a normal mother and grandmother, he'd be married with two or three kids by now. Instead, he survived on a series of short-lived affairs with women who seemed perfectly normal at first, but who strangely always ended up unsuitable or unstable.

When Eli finally emerged from the bathroom, dressed in the cargo pants and T-shirt, Annalise was waiting in the hallway with a hot cup of tea. She pulled him along to the kitchen table and shoved a stack of shoe boxes off a chair and onto the floor. "Sit, sit. When Vanessa called, I was so surprised. I wasn't expecting you. Usually you call."

"I didn't really have a chance," he said, picking up a pair of climbing shoes that she'd pushed aside. "Do these come in my size?"

She smiled. Though she'd reached the half-century mark last year, Annalise Montgomery still had a girl-ish exuberance that belied her true age. Her slender body, kept healthy by yoga and a vegan diet, moved with a grace and athleticism that made her hard to ignore.

"Richard Baskill?" he said.

"Oh, stop. I don't need you to tell me who I can and cannot screw." She sat down across from him and tucked her feet up under her. "It's just a thing. An undeniable sexual attraction. I'm going through menopause and they say sometimes women just freak out and try to do it with any man who walks by." She shrugged, a coy grin twitching at the corners of her lips. "So I did. And I'll have you know, he's quite an accomplished lover. Besides, there's nothing left to do about the resort. He managed to buy every politician that could have stopped it. I just figured it was time to go with the flow."

"So the next best thing was to hop into bed with him?"

She giggled. "We actually haven't done it in a bed yet. He likes it when I get…creative. I couldn't beat him with the resort, but I do hold all the power in the bedroom."

Eli covered his ears. "Too much information," he shouted, shaking his head.

"All right, all right," she said, grabbing his hand and lacing her fingers through his. "No more talk about my love life. Let's talk about yours."

"There's nothing to talk about," Eli said.

She gave him a sad look and sighed.

"Is there some kind of sexual dysfunction that keeps you from—"

"Stop!" Eli said. "I'm not going to talk to you about my sex life."

A silence descended and she busied herself braiding a strand of her hair. As much as he loved his mother's rather mercurial personality, it often made simple conversation nearly impossible. She usually blurted out exactly what was on her mind, without the benefit of a filter. Though, truth be told, Eli had come to the conclusion that she enjoyed shocking people.

"Is there some other topic we might discuss?" Eli asked.

"I suppose your inability to settle down and find a purpose for your life is off-limits as well?"

"The commitment gene is missing in the Montgomery family," he muttered. "I take after you and

Trudie. I make enough money to live my life. That's all I need for now."

"Well, in the interest of making money to live your life, I just happen to have a job for you, a good-paying job. They hired me to do it, but now that you're home, I think you'd be perfect for it."

"What kind of job?"

"I got a call from a production company in Los Angeles. They're doing a reality show, a girl-in-the-wild thing where they drop this woman into the wilderness and she has to fend for herself for a year. They wanted to rent Trudie's cabin because they're basing the concept on her life on the mountain."

"You rented out my grandmother's cabin?"

"You won't believe what they paid," Annalise said. "It's all very professional. This woman they got to host the show, Lucy Parker, she's read all your grandmother's books. She's a huge fan."

"How old is she?"

"What difference does that make? I was twenty-four when I first climbed Everest. Your grandmother was fifty when she wrote her first book. Age is just another metric that men use to put women down."

Eli cursed softly. "All right, never mind her age. How long is she going to live there all alone? Two, three months?"

"A year. And she isn't alone. She has a dog with her."

"A year? How is a TV personality from Los Angeles going to feed herself? Does she hunt? What about chopping wood? There must be a production crew that's going to stay with her. They wouldn't leave her up there all alone." He stared at Annalise. "Well? Did you ask these questions?"

"Well…no. I'm sure they know what they're doing."

"Does she have a radio or a sat phone to call if she needs help?"

His mother shrugged. "I have no idea. You can find out yourself when you hike up there the day after tomorrow. That's the job. Check up on her once a month. Bring a few supplies to her." She stood up. "In the meantime, I think we should go out and stuff ourselves with pizza and beer."

"You don't eat cheese," he said. "You're a vegan."

"I've realized that cheese is quite possibly the most sublime food on the planet. And I only eat organic cheese from grass-fed, humanely pastured milk cows."

"Next thing you'll be telling me that you're eating meat."

"Bacon," she said. "I mean, it's really not meat. It's fat. And it smells like sex feels. At my age, I just don't think I should deny any of my urges. Life is short. We have to enjoy every single moment. That's what Richard says."

Eli rubbed his forehead, wondering at the sudden knot of tension beneath his fingertips. Maybe a beer—or five—was exactly what he needed right now. It appeared that a lot of things had changed since he'd last been home.

Leave it to his mother to involve them both in some silly reality show. The *reality* was that life in Trudie's cabin was hard and lonely and it wasn't a place for make-believe adventurers. He intended to let Lucy

Parker know exactly what she was in for. And once she found out what a winter in the Rockies would be like, she'd want to run right back down the mountain.

LUCY PARKER ROLLED over on her bunk and winced at the ache in her shoulder. She'd spent the previous day stripping the bark from a tree she'd felled last week. It was backbreaking work, but all part of the process—the process of building her own shelter that would withstand the harsh winter.

She sat up and brushed the hair out of her eyes. This was the life she'd signed on for. A year in the wilderness, a year living life as Trudie Montgomery had. And the first task was to construct a small log cabin. She'd been on the mountain for exactly a month and had managed to gather enough logs for one wall of the ten-by-ten foot shelter she'd planned to build.

Her plans had undergone some revisions once she realized how heavy a twelve-foot tree could be. So she'd reduced the diameter of the trees she harvested to only those she could drag through the woods herself.

Though she was behind schedule, Lucy was certain that once her body got used to the specific labors involved, she'd pick up speed.

Her only companion in this adventure, her dog, Riley, was stretched out beside her on the old iron bed. When she sat up, he lifted his head. "I'd sleep much better if you'd stay on your side," she muttered. He gave her a soft woof then leaped over her and scurried to the door.

She crawled out of bed, wrapping the old quilt around her to ward off the chill, then opened the front door of the cabin. Her breath caught in her throat as she took in the amazing landscape around her. To the west were mountains—high, craggy, snow-covered peaks. To the east, thick forest and the foothills. The closest town was Stone Creek, twenty miles away by air, but hours by vehicle and foot. She'd come to the cabin via a helicopter that had landed in the wide green meadow to the south, a meadow now painted in the watercolor hues of the first wildflowers of the season.

Riley scratched at the screen door and she opened it. He ran out and she followed at a more leisurely pace. She'd put her watch away and sealed it in an old baking-powder tin, allowing her body to dictate the hours of the day. When she was hungry, she ate. When she was tired, she slept. And when it was time to work, she focused all her energy to push herself harder than she'd ever been pushed. She loved it.

Lucy drew a deep breath of the crisp morning air. Her year in the wild promised to be both a personal and a professional challenge, and she relished the chance to prove herself. She'd bounced around from job to job in television production for years, picking up jobs where she could and making enough to put herself through college. She'd read Trudie's books when she was a teenager and had dreamed of a life spent alone, with nothing but her strength and wits to sustain her.

An offhand conversation with another producer had resulted in a proposal for a new reality show. She'd spend a year in the wilderness, following in the footsteps of famous feminist Trudie Montgomery. Amazingly, her proposal had been accepted, a production budget had been secured and on April first, Lucy had been left in the meadow with Riley and twenty crates of supplies to get her through the next twelve months.

All she had to do was provide at least fifteen hours of video footage per week, chronicling her efforts to survive in the wilderness, recording her thoughts on Trudie, her feminist ideals and the challenges she'd faced. Meanwhile, the producers were working to sell the series to a network.

Lucy had been given a battery-operated two-way radio to call for help in case of an emergency, a laptop computer with a satellite uplink to upload her video footage each week and a generator to charge both the video camera and laptop.

Figuring it should be charged now, she walked back inside and grabbed the video camera, then sat down on the top porch step and turned it toward herself. Pushing the record button, she smiled. "Hooray, hooray, it's the third of May. I've been on the mountain for exactly one month and today, I'm going to have a visitor. Annalise Montgomery, Trudie's daughter, has agreed to stop by once a month to check up on me and bring me a few supplies. And to chat with us. Those of you who've read Trudie's books know that Trudie's friend and lover, Buck Garrison, used to stop by every month with necessities, but there will be no men visiting me."

Rachel McFarlane and Anna Conners, her two producers, had decided that the entire project, from production on down, should be run by women. The pair had produced an award-winning PBS special on the all-women's America's Cup racing crew several years before and were certain that it would be a positive message to send to the public and a good way to market the show to the networks when it came time to sell it.

"What do I need?" Lucy continued. "A few extra lanterns for the very dark mountain nights. Another pair of long underwear. Some heavier socks. And a new washboard to do laundry. I could also use some chocolate, but I didn't put that on my list as I've decided to go cold turkey." She paused. "Turkey. I'd also love a turkey sandwich. Canned meat has already lost its appeal."

Riley's bark caught her attention and Lucy trained the lens on the meadow, hoping to catch Annalise as she approached. In the distance, she made out a lone figure moving toward her. She tried to make out the details of Annalise's face, then sucked in a sharp breath.

It wasn't the slender figure of Annalise, but a tall, lanky man who approached. She noticed the rifle slung over his shoulder. He also carried a large frame pack, yet moved as if it weighed nothing.

Lucy had been in the wilderness for an entire month and this was the first visitor she'd had. Though she felt a small measure of excitement, this wasn't the person she'd expected. Calling for Riley, she motioned the dog to her side and he sat down, his attention now fixed on the stranger. As the man approached the cabin, Lucy observed him more closely.

He was tall and broad-shouldered, wearing hiking shorts and boots, a faded T-shirt, sunglasses and a cap that shaded his eyes. Thick, dark hair curled out from under the cap and the shadow of a beard darkened his face.

A tiny tremor raced through her. There was a reason why the production company had hired Annalise Montgomery to make the monthly visits, beyond the show's premise. After a month of solitude, a single man—hell, any man—caused a riot of unsettling feelings inside of her, even if he might be a backwoods ax murderer.

Lucy suddenly realized how vulnerable she was, out here all alone. She set the camera down and grabbed the rifle from its spot just inside the door. Nestling the butt into her shoulder, she got the man in her sights. "Stop right there," she shouted across the twenty yards that separated them. Riley growled softly.

Startled, he did as he was ordered, slowly raising his hands and watching her suspiciously. "Are you really planning to use that?" he shouted.

"I will if I have to."

"Then nestle the stock into your shoulder and raise the muzzle up. Unless your intended target is the dirt five feet in front of me. Don't tell me they didn't even teach you to shoot properly."

"What are you doing here?"

"The more appropriate question," he muttered, starting toward her again, "would be what are *you* doing here?" He dropped his hands to the straps on his pack and hooked his thumbs beneath them.

She narrowed her gaze. "Who are you?"

"Annalise sent me," he said. "I've brought some supplies. And I guess I'm supposed to make sure you haven't done anything stupid, like starve to death or get eaten by a bear. You look healthy and I don't see any teeth marks, so I assume you're all right so far?"

Lucy stifled a smile as she set the gun down beside her. She stepped off the porch, suddenly curious about the man who'd wandered into her orbit. He slipped the pack off his back, then stretched his arms above his head. Then, in one smooth movement, he pulled his T-shirt over his head and used it to wipe the perspiration from his face.

Lucy bit back a moan as she took in his finely muscled chest and impossibly sculpted abdomen. Her fingers twitched as she imagined running her hands over the tanned skin, pressing her lips to the smooth expanse of naked skin.

This was crazy. She'd gone far longer than a month without a man in her life before. Why was she reacting so strongly to this guy now? Yes, he was gorgeous. And she hadn't had any human contact for a month. But she should be able to control her reactions much better than this.

He cleared his throat and when she met his gaze, Lucy realized she'd been caught staring. "You shouldn't be here," she murmured. "Annalise agreed to come."

"She thought I'd enjoy the fresh air and a good, long hike."

"We had an agreement," Lucy said.

"Well, if you knew anything about Annalise you'd understand that she's rather flexible when it comes to promises and agreements."

"We have a contract. This entire project is supposed to be run by women. Women producers, women editors. We want to make a statement. Exactly how Trudie would have wanted it."

"How do you know what Trudie wanted?" he asked. "You never even met her."

"And I suppose you did?" she asked, arching her eyebrow and leveling a cool gaze at him.

"I used to spend summers here with her," he said. "I helped her put up the addition on the cabin and I built that outhouse all by myself."

Her breath caught in her throat. Annalise had mentioned that she had a son, but she said he was away a lot and that they didn't see much of each other. Cursing beneath her breath, she strode up to him and held out her hand. "You must be—"

"Eli," he said after studying her for a long, uncomfortable moment. "Eli Montgomery. I'm Annalise's son."

"I'm Lucy Parker," she said, sending him an apologetic smile. Of course the son of a woman like Annalise would be as handsome as she was beautiful. And he'd have to love the outdoors.

He took her hand in his and gave it a shake.

"It's a pleasure to meet you," she said.

He took off his sunglasses, letting them hang from the strap around his neck, and she found herself transfixed by eyes so blue, they rivaled the sky above. They stared at each other warily, like two wild animals deciding between fight or flight.

"You must have left very early to get here before noon," she said.

"I move fast," he said.

A shiver skittered down her spine and she drew her fingers from his.

"For most people, it's a four-hour hike," he explained. "I can do it in three. And if I'm going to make the round trip before sunset, I wanted to be here by noon."

"You're going to leave right away?"

He frowned. "Yeah. I guess I didn't think you'd want me to stick around. Why? You need something? You want me to stay?"

"No, no. You're right. You really should go. The whole point of this project is for me to live life like Trudie did."

"Trudie had lots of visitors," he said.

"In that case, maybe you could you stay for lunch?" She gave him a tentative smile. "To be honest, it would be nice to have some company. Even for just an hour. And as long as you don't do any of the cooking, I guess it won't break any rules."

"There are rules?"

"Guidelines, really. An entire notebook filled with them. I can't accept any outside help, beyond the monthly check-in."

"All right," he said. "I'll stay. Under one condition."

"What would that be?"

"You let me show you how to handle that rifle."

"I know how to handle it. They gave me lessons at a shooting range in LA."

"Even so, I'd like to show you myself."

Lucy sighed. "All right. We'll do that after lunch." She glanced down at what she was wearing, realizing for the first time that she must look like some kind of crazy lady. "I'm just going to get dressed. Is there anything you need? I can—" Lucy paused. "I guess you remember where everything is. Just make yourself comfortable."

She hurried back inside the cabin and slammed the door behind her. Leaning against the rough planks, she drew a deep breath. "Stop it!" she muttered. This was ridiculous.

She'd come here, to this remote mountain cabin, to prove that a woman didn't need a man to find peace and contentment in the world. And here she was, panting over Eli Montgomery like he'd come specifically to seduce her.

He was delivering supplies and nothing more. Just because he had a nice smile and a charming manner did not mean he wanted to pick her up, wrap her legs around his waist and do the nasty.

"Show some self-control," Lucy said to herself, pushing off the door.

Still, as she searched the cabin for something decent to wear, she discarded anything that might make her look lumpy. In the end, she settled for yoga pants and a simple chambray shirt that she knotted at the waist.

For the first time since she arrived, she regretted the lack of a mirror in the cabin. It was something that Trudie had prided herself on—the ability to grow comfortable with her natural appearance. Lucy grabbed a brush and quickly ran it through her hair. "Forgive me, Trudie," she murmured, pinching her cheeks to give herself a bit of color.

When she opened the door again, Eli was sitting on the porch, Riley stretched out beside him. He'd unpacked the supplies he'd brought along, laying them out on the floor. "Is that chocolate?" she asked.

"It is. My mother thought you might need it, but I can take it back down with me if you don't want it."

She reached down and grabbed the package of chocolate bars. "Not a chance, mister. Now, if you'd also brought me a triple-shot caramel latte, I might have kissed you."

"Nope," he said with a grin. "But I'll remember that next month."

ELI HADN'T PLANNED to spend any time at the cabin. He'd been irritated that his mother had rented out the property, especially for a dumb reality television show, and he wasn't really looking forward to meeting the new tenant. But then he'd gotten a good look at Lucy Parker.

He'd expected some fortysomething feminist, a woman experienced with life and ready to prove a point to anyone who might be interested. He'd imagined someone like his grandmother, not some sweet-faced, doe-eyed woman with a disarming smile and an amazing body.

It was clear why they'd picked her for the job. Even dressed in raggedy clothes with her hair tangled, she was drop-dead beautiful. She wasn't wearing a bit of makeup to enhance her features and yet, she had a beauty that was unmatched by any woman he'd ever met.

Her skin was flawless, pale and smooth, and her lips were as pink as ripening fruit. Her hair, thick and flaxen in color, tumbled around her face in a style that was best reserved for the bedroom immediately after sex.

Eli had been prepared to hate her, or at least dislike her for underestimating the harsh reality of living on the mountain. But she was so determined to honor Trudie with this project that he found himself carried along by her enthusiasm. Still, he was worried about her preparedness. Before he could walk away, he needed to know that she'd be fine out here all by herself.

In the meantime, he tried his best to ignore the attraction pulsing between them. She'd made it very clear that the last thing she wanted was a man. He wouldn't be chopping her firewood, he wouldn't be digging her garden and he wouldn't be warming her bed. But maybe there was one thing he could do for her.

He picked up the sandwich that Lucy had made for him and took a bite. The rustic bread was freshly baked and she'd slathered homemade hummus on it, flavored with garlic and roasted red peppers. "This is delicious," he said.

"Thanks." She pulled her knees up beneath her chin. "I put a lot of time and effort into my menu. If I think a lot about food, I can contain my cravings."

"And what do you crave?" he asked. "Besides a caramel latte? And chocolate?"

"Potato chips. Ice cream. Pizza. I dream about pizza."

"Well, you're about an eight-hour hike from a really great pizza parlor. Maybe you could get them to deliver," he teased.

"I expected to miss food. And all my electronics. Television and movies. But what I really miss is people. It's so quiet here at night it almost makes my

ears hurt. I don't know what I'd do without Riley."
She drew a deep breath. "And fruit. I miss fresh fruit."

"There will be places you can get that around here
later this summer," he said. "About a mile in that direction are two apple trees that were planted near the
foundation of an old cabin. And over there, along that
ridge, are blackberry bushes, but watch out for bears
because they like them as much as humans do. There
are also wild plum and boysenberry trees nearby.
Trudie used to make the best jam."

He wanted to show her, to tell her everything that
he knew to help her survive and make her stay more
bearable. But he remembered her very strict set of
rules. "I'd draw you a map, but you'd probably rip it
up and throw it in the fire."

She nodded, then pushed to her feet. "Is there anything else I can get you?"

He wanted to ask if she'd let him run his fingers
through her hair, or smooth his hand over her cheek.
He wanted to stare into her eyes and memorize the
color so he might recall it later. Most of all, he wanted
to kiss her and see if the attraction he felt was mutual or just some silly fantasy that he was experiencing on his own.

"Get me your rifle," he said. "And bring a box of
ammunition."

"What are you going to shoot?" she said, glancing
around. "Is there a bear?"

"No. We're just going to have a little target practice," he said. "Humor me. I want to be sure you *could*
shoot a bear if you had to."

Lucy grudgingly produced the rifle. She was
clearly not happy with him for forcing the issue but

she was smart enough to realize that a little extra instruction with the rifle could save her life if she did encounter a bear or some other wild animal.

Over the next half hour, they set up targets in the meadow, nailing flattened tin cans to the trunks of aspen trees.

"I am curious about that pile of logs over there," Eli said, nodding to the west of the cabin. "I notice you've been stripping them. They'll burn fine with the bark."

"Those aren't for the fire. I'm building a cabin."

Eli chuckled. "No, really."

"Really," she said. "Your grandmother built this cabin all on her own. I want to do the same."

"Yes, she built it. Over the course of two or three summers. With the help of friends and two horses."

"I don't have any horses," she said. "And I don't have friends. But that doesn't mean I'm not going to try."

Eli tacked a tin can to the tree trunk, shaking his head. "Do you have any idea what you're doing out here? You seem to have some kind of delusion—or maybe it's a fantasy—of what wilderness life is like." He continued on to the next tree.

"I have your grandmother's books," she said, hurrying after him. "And I've done my homework. I know it's difficult, but that only makes me more determined to do it."

"To what end? Trudie already proved that it was possible. Why do you need to build a cabin all over again? Is it meant to make you famous?" He held out his hand and she gave him another tin can. "How the hell did you get these logs here?"

"I dragged them," she said.

He stared at her in disbelief.

"I have to find just the right circumference and length. I was going to make a fourteen-by-fourteen cabin like your grandmother, but those logs are too heavy. So I've reduced it to ten-by-ten and I'm using six-inch diameter logs." She held up her hand. "I know. It'll take more logs, but I'm going to do it. And for your information, it has nothing to do with being famous. I'm doing this for myself."

Eli couldn't help but admire her tenacity. The process she described was brutal and backbreaking. He grabbed her hands and turned them over, only to see the shadows of healed blisters and new calluses. He ran his thumbs over the rough surface and he heard her take a ragged breath.

"You need a pair of gloves," he said.

She nodded. "I have a pair but they don't fit very well. And I accidentally left them out in the rain."

Eli gently massaged her palm and his blood warmed. When he looked up and met her wide-eyed gaze, he realized what he was doing and dropped her hand. "You have a lot of work to do if you're going to finish it before the first snow," he said

"I can do it," Lucy said. "I'm learning more every day and getting better at each of the tasks."

"Can I give you some advice?" he asked.

She shook her head. "No. You can't. It would be… cheating."

"This isn't a game, princess," he said. "I don't see any referees around here."

"I am *going* to do this on my own. I want the project to have integrity. I need to make my own mistakes."

"It will be a costly mistake when you drag logs through thick underbrush because you didn't want to let me tell you to get your logs cut and hauled early."

She clapped her hands to her ears and shook her head, sending him an angry glare. "No!"

He cursed softly and shook his head. "Listen, I'm dead serious. The last thing I want to do is hike up here and find the vultures picking at your carcass. I know that's crude, but it's a reality in the mountains, especially when you're alone."

"I'm careful. And prepared."

"Then let's see it." He strode over to where he'd left the rifle and shells and walked back to her. "Pace it off. We'll start with twenty paces."

He followed her as she did as he ordered, then stood behind her. "If you come across a bear, stop and keep your eyes on the ground. Slowly bring your gun around, but keep it pointed down. Do that for me now."

He placed his hands on her shoulders, squaring her body to the target. But the moment he touched her, he realized his mistake. Suddenly, he couldn't focus on the shooting lesson. Instead, he was fascinated by the warm flesh beneath the fabric of her shirt and the gentle curve between her shoulder and neck. The scent of her hair drifted on the breeze and he closed his eyes for a moment, trying to identify the floral variety.

"When you bring your rifle up, it's important to stabilize it by pulling the butt into your shoulder with your cheek against the stock. Same place every time, nice and solid. If you do that, sighting your target shouldn't take long."

He reached around her and showed her how to hold the gun. His blood surged and his pulse quickened, but he forced himself to ignore the reaction and focus on the job at hand.

"Now, sight the target and when you have it, squeeze the trigger."

A few seconds later, a shot exploded out of the muzzle and Lucy winced. "Did I hit it?"

"Nope."

"But I always hit the target at the range."

"Shooting at the range is a lot different than shooting when a bear is charging you. Or even with the wind blowing and the trees rustling. That can is about the size of the spot you need to hit to down a bear."

"But it's so small from back here."

"Any closer to the target, you won't have time to get a shot off."

Eli glanced at his watch. It was almost three. The hike out would be quicker as it was downhill and he'd have an empty pack, but it would still be tight. And he hadn't brought along a headlamp, so he had to reach the ATV before sunset. "I have to get going. But I want you to practice this after I leave. Every day. Until you can hit those cans in the blink of an eye."

Lucy slowly turned. "Thank you," she said.

His gaze fell to her lips and he fought the urge to lean forward and take a taste. "No problem. I wish we could work on it some more, but then I'd have to spend the night. I'm sure that's against the rules." He wasn't sure what had possessed him to practically beg for an invitation, and he wanted to take the words back the moment he said them.

"Guidelines," she corrected. "They're really just guidelines. But I plan to follow them as if they were laws."

They walked back to the cabin together and Eli retrieved his pack and slipped the straps over his shoulders. "Well, Lucy Parker, I guess this is goodbye, then. Have a great year and stay safe."

"Won't I see you next month?" she asked.

"What about your law? I thought a man was against the rules," he said.

"You won't be helping me with the cabin. And I don't want to put Annalise out if she's busy."

"Then I'll see you next month," he said.

Lucy smiled, then pushed up on her toes and brushed a quick kiss across his cheek. "Thanks again. I enjoyed our visit."

He smoothed his hand along her arm and caught her hand in his. "If I kissed you," he murmured, "would that be against the guidelines?"

"It definitely would," she said.

Eli nodded, the conflict between his common sense and his impulses raging on in his head. In the end, he stepped back, gradually moving away from her, their gazes still locked. "Stay safe," he said, giving her a halfhearted wave.

She waved back and he turned and headed across the meadow toward the trailhead. Eli looked over his shoulder once and found her still watching him from the porch, her arms wrapped around the post, her hair tossed by the breeze. Riley sat at her feet, his head resting on his paws.

Eli tried to forget her the moment she was out of sight. But instead, she plagued his thoughts for the entire hike down the mountain, then the ride back into town and through the rest of his night. He'd almost convinced himself that it was simple worry that kept her on his mind. After all, she was a vulnerable young woman, alone in the wilderness with no one to protect her. He couldn't just leave her to fend for herself.

But when his dreams turned into scorching sexual fantasies of naked limbs entwined and wild sensations racing through his body, Eli knew protecting Lucy wasn't the only reason he wanted to go back to the cabin.

2

June

LUCY TICKED OFF the days on her calendar as the first of June approached. Though she'd tried to tell herself that it would be Annalise checking in, she held out hope that it would be Eli instead.

She couldn't help but feel guilty over the attraction that had consumed her for the past month. After all, this whole experience was about finding the strength in being a woman. But instead the only thing she could think about was Eli Montgomery. He was just so…handsome and charming. And dangerous.

He was exactly the kind of man who could lure a woman into an affair without a second thought to what she might be giving up for him. The problem was, the more time Lucy spent alone, the more she seemed to dwell on sex.

It wasn't just a nagging desire that came and went. She seemed to be obsessed with thoughts of raging passion and unfulfilled need, quite unusual for her. And the male subject in every one of these fantasies just happened to be Eli Montgomery, mysterious mountain man and destroyer of feminist ideals. It was a problem she'd never anticipated.

She'd been pacing the cabin for most of the morning, busying herself with bread-making and an attempt to make a vegan mac and cheese. After two months in the wild, she'd added dairy products to her list of things she'd begun to crave.

She opened the oven to check on the bread, then realized that she'd left it in too long. "Damn," she muttered, grabbing a dishtowel and a potholder. Gauging the temperature of her wood-burning oven was an art that she'd not yet mastered.

She pulled the two pans out, setting the first on top of the stove and searching for an empty spot on the counter for the second. But the heat of the pan seeped through the towel and she screamed as she dropped it on the floor, the loaf tumbling out of the pan to land in front of a pair of well-worn hiking boots.

Lucy glanced up to see Eli watching her through the screen door. Either he'd left before sunrise or he'd run up the mountainside. It was barely ten and she looked as if she'd just crawled out of bed.

He opened the door and stepped inside, then bent down and grabbed the loaf of bread. "I think you dropped this," he murmured, his gaze slowly drifting down to her mouth.

Lucy groaned inwardly. So he'd come back. Had it been his choice or had Annalise had another conflict in her schedule?

"Thanks," she said, grabbing the bread with the towel, then slowly straightening. She was dressed in a faded T-shirt and nothing else. Thankfully, the T-shirt nearly reached her knees. "You're early."

"I figured you might need a hand with a few things, so I gave myself some extra time to help you."

She shook her head. "I can't—"

"I know, I know. But I thought maybe after two months on your own, you might have changed your mind."

"Nope," she said. "I haven't changed my mind."

He grinned, then turned and grabbed his pack from just outside the front door. He pulled a thermos from the side pocket and held it out to her. "Then you probably don't want this, either."

Lucy regarded the stainless-steel container suspiciously. "What's that?"

"Caramel latte. Triple shot, I believe. Still hot. As I recall, you requested it the last time I was here. I'm just following orders."

Lucy smiled. She *had* told him that she'd been craving her favorite coffee drink. And she'd also promised a kiss in exchange. But she'd just been joking.

"Maybe there's a rule against drinking it, though," he said. "If there is, I'll just dump it."

She reached for it, then drew her hand back when she recalled her promise. "And what do you expect in return?"

"I believe you promised a kiss." He handed her the thermos. "But since it's my job to look after you, I won't demand payment." He paused. "Yet."

She wanted to kiss him. It was all she'd been thinking about for the past month. Maybe getting it over with would satisfy her hormones and allow her to move on. So why not just go for it? What did she have to lose? He'd be leaving again in a few hours, and at least she'd have some real-world experience to add to her fantasies.

Lucy took the thermos from his hand and smiled. She stepped up to him, wrapped her hand around his nape and gave him a sweet, slow kiss. But then he slipped his hand around her waist and pulled her closer, and a tiny cry of surprise burst from between her lips.

The moment he touched her, the tenuous hold on her self-control vanished. He deepened the kiss, his tongue gently tasting until her body melted into his. Lucy thought the kiss would go on forever, but then he loosened his hold and she stumbled back.

When she met his gaze again, he was smiling at her. "Judging by that kiss, I'd assume there was a major rewrite on those guidelines of yours within the last month."

"I was…just paying a debt," she said. "For the coffee?"

"Wait till you see what else I have in my pack, then," he said.

"Why don't you unpack it on the porch?" she suggested. "I'll be out in a few minutes."

When he'd closed the door behind him, Lucy walked over to the bed and sat down on the edge. She touched her lips, still damp from his kiss, then flopped back and stared up at the ceiling.

She'd accepted this project because she'd been intrigued by the challenge, at least that's what she'd said whenever she was asked or interviewed. But it was also a way to live an entire year in one place.

She couldn't remember the last time that had happened. Her childhood had been spent in a series of foster homes, none of which she'd stayed in longer than six months. At fourteen, she'd run away from a bad foster family and ended up on the streets. She'd managed to survive there for two years before she'd gotten a job and started bringing in a paycheck. After that she'd bounced from one cheap room to another.

Sometimes, she'd slept on friends' couches or took a house-sitting job. Then, when she'd gotten a full-time gig with a production company, she was often on location. But here, on the mountain, she had a chance to live in a home, rugged as it might be.

Working in television and movie production had always been a perfect job for her. She'd enjoyed the shifting scenery, a new location every few months. But the past year or two, she'd started to wonder if her lifestyle was keeping her from finding contentment in her life.

The cabin wasn't just a home. It was place for her to settle. She'd hoped that a year on her own, alone in the wilderness, might give her time to figure out her future. Who was she? Where did she belong? Was this the only life she was destined to live or was there something else waiting for her?

Lucy thought she'd have at least a few answers by now. But the longer she stayed on the mountain, the more confused she became. The only thing she knew for sure, at this very moment, was that she wanted to spend the day enjoying the company of Eli Montgomery. They had the next five hours together and she was going to make the most of them.

Lucy crawled off the bed and quickly dressed, then

found her brush and pulled it through her tangled hair. She hadn't had a real bath or a shower since the day before she arrived at the cabin, but she'd scrubbed herself clean last night with a bar of homemade soap and six pots of water she'd heated on the stove.

When she opened the door again, she found Eli sitting on the top step, petting Riley. She grabbed a couple enamel coffee mugs and sat down next to him, then poured out the contents of the thermos he'd brought. The scents of caramel and coffee wafted in the morning air and she groaned softly. "You were very sweet to remember," she said after taking a slow sip.

"I was just interested in that kiss," he said.

She clasped her hands around the mug. "I was really expecting your mother this time. Was she busy again?"

"No, I wanted to come. I thought I should check up on your shooting. And bring you coffee."

"I'm glad you came. I mean, it would have been fine if Annalise had come. She's just amazing and—"

"Amazing and insane," he murmured.

"Why would you say that?"

"She's been dating this real estate developer, whom she hated until recently, and she's acting like a lovesick teenager. I told her to seek professional help. She said I could use a father figure in my life."

"Where is your father, if that's not too personal of a question?" she asked.

Eli shrugged. "I never knew him. My mother raised me on her own. I found out who he was when I was fifteen, but by that time it was too late."

"Too late?"

"He'd died in a climbing accident several years before. On Mount Everest. He left behind a loving wife and four legitimate children—and me. I was the result of a brief fling he had with my mother in a tent during some climbing expedition."

"And you never met him?"

"Once, apparently. My mother claims that she took me to New Zealand when I was six and I met him then. I don't remember it, though. It's always been just me and Annalise. And Trudie. And my grandfather, Buck."

"That's a family," she said. "That's a pretty big family, by my standards."

"What about you?"

"I had a happy childhood," she lied. "Nothing extraordinary. My parents are still married, living in Seattle. My dad works for the post office and my mom is a teacher. I'm an only child."

It was a complete and utter fabrication, but she'd told the story so many times that it sounded true. It was just detailed enough that it didn't cause additional questions and just vague enough that it was instantly forgettable.

"How did you end up here, in the middle of nowhere, building a log cabin with your bare hands?"

"I was sixteen and wandering around the streets of Seattle during the summer, bored with my life, and came across a production company. They were filming a movie and I asked if they might have a job for me, and they did. I was an outstanding coffee fetcher. After that, I was hooked. I worked a few more local productions and built up a decent résumé. When I graduated from high school, I took a bus to LA and found better work. I went to college when I could, and I've been on some kind of TV or movie production set ever since. I pitched this series after I reread one of your grandmother's books. The producers asked if I wanted to be in front of the camera and I said yes."

It was a simple enough explanation and one she'd given to almost everyone she'd met over the course of the past year. This part of the story was entirely true, though she'd left out a few major details. But the real truth would probably come out when the show was broadcast. Someone would recognize her and reveal the truth about her past.

The world would find out that her father had gone to prison when she was seven and her mother had died of a drug overdose when she was five. They'd know about the foster homes and the constant running away, living on the streets when she was fourteen and searching for any way to make a few dollars to feed herself. She'd been one of the lucky ones. She'd been smart and resourceful. And she'd always been a credible liar.

"So you came here because of Trudie?"

"Yeah. She was such a strong woman and wanted to experience life on her own terms, stripped down, simple. I remember reading her book about building the cabin and how she lived off the grid. I was always fascinated by that concept of creating a life for yourself out of nothing but your own two hands."

"I wish you could have met her."

"Me, too. But you can tell me about her." She took another sip of her coffee. "Now that you've finished interrogating me, why don't you show me what you brought?"

Eli turned to his pack and the first thing he pulled out was a pair of deerskin gloves. He held them out to her. "These should fit a bit better than what you've been wearing. You won't get so many blisters."

She stared down at the gloves and a flood of emotion washed over her—he'd remembered. For the first time in her life, she felt as if someone was listening to her. He'd done her a great kindness. That kind of thing rarely happened in her life. And now, he'd done it twice—first, the coffee and now the gloves.

Was this the beginning of a friendship…or a passionate affair? Lucy wasn't sure which one she wanted more, but she had no idea how to handle either.

"TELL ME EVERYTHING you know about bears."

"Why are you so obsessed with bears?" Lucy asked.

"Because they are an always-present danger up here once the snow melts. If it were winter, I'd be obsessed with hypothermia."

They walked through the meadow together toward the tree line, their rifles slung over their shoulders, Riley trotting beside them. Eli had decided that if she wouldn't take advice about cabin building and food foraging, he was going to make damn sure she kept herself safe. And for the next couple of months, the biggest threat in this part of the mountains was the bears.

"I know to carry my gun at all times. I've been practicing on the targets almost every day. I know that I'll probably only have time for one shot and if it's not good, the bear will probably eat me for dinner. Avoidance is the best strategy."

"Excellent. Anything else?"

"Keep Riley and all food locked up in the cabin when I'm not around. Hungry bears are dangerous. Mother bears with their cubs are the most dangerous. Black bears are usually afraid of humans, grizzlies are more aggressive."

"And what if a bear does charge?" he asked.

"With a grizzly, you drop to the ground and curl up and protect your neck and head. Basically play dead. With a black bear, you run or fight back as hard as you can. You make noise, throw rocks, hit him with sticks."

He nodded. "All right. There's not much chance you'll run into a grizzly around here. They range farther north. But I will give you this." He pulled a can out of his pocket. "Bear pepper spray. A temporarily blinded bear is much better than a wounded bear." He reached down and clipped it to her jeans. "If you can't get a shot off or if you just wound him, use the spray and run like hell."

"Thanks," she said.

"Just don't use that on me the next time I try to kiss you," he teased.

"Are you planning to kiss me again?" she asked.

There was the question, Eli mused. After their first kiss, he hadn't been able to stop thinking about his next excuse to kiss her again. There was no use trying to ignore the attraction. Now that he knew it was mutual, Eli didn't see any reason to keep his hands— or his lips—to himself.

It might have been different if it had really been a month since he'd last seen her. But Eli had hiked up to the meadow once a week just to make sure she was all right. At first, he'd tried to convince himself he was just checking on the cabin. Then, he'd convinced himself that the production company should have specified weekly visits and he was correcting their error.

But as he'd sat on the edge of the meadow, hidden by the brush, and saw her work on the cabin or practice her shooting, he realized that he just needed to know that she was safe. Lucy wasn't like his mother or grandmother. She was a city girl, and he'd glimpsed a vulnerability in her that he couldn't ignore. He'd witnessed it again and again over the years—amateurs who traveled to remote locations convinced they were prepared, but who ended up sick or injured. Even his father, an experienced climber, had made one mistake and had never come down the mountain. He wouldn't let that happen to Lucy. It had become his duty to protect her and one he would never shirk.

Last week, Riley had caught his scent and he'd had to run to avoid being discovered. And it was always difficult to walk away. He'd considered just hiking to the cabin and making up some excuse for his presence. But Eli knew better. When it came to Lucy, it was best to follow the rules—or the *guidelines*.

They walked along a familiar ridgeline, then dropped down to hike a narrow creek bed. It had been years since Eli had explored this part of his grandmother's world, but the landmarks he'd used were still deeply etched in his memory.

"Where are we going?" she asked.

"Haven't you been paying attention?"

"No, I was following you."

He reached back and grabbed his water bottle, then

took a long drink before holding it out to her. "I guess we're lost then."

Her eyes went wide. "How could we be lost? I assumed you knew where you were going." She stared at him for a long moment, then shook her head. "Oh, I get it. This is another lesson from Captain Safety."

"Maybe you should get out that video camera of yours. This is important stuff."

She slipped her pack off her shoulder and set it at her feet, then removed the camera. "I'm not going to be able to use this footage," she said.

"No, but you can watch it when I'm gone."

Lucy trained the lens on him. "Then take off your shirt," she teased, focusing on the broad expanse of his chest. "It will make the video much more interesting."

"I'm serious," he said.

"So am I," she countered.

He watched her as she toyed with the camera, his gaze fixed on her lips, his thoughts focused on the last kiss they'd shared. There were more than a few consequences that came along with kissing Lucy again. Especially kissing her for nothing but the pleasure of it.

She'd come to the mountain for some kind of feminist empowerment deal, and the last thing he wanted to do was interfere in her professional or personal goals. Then there was the whole guilt thing. If he ruined her life with romance, she'd blame him for wrecking her project. And he wasn't usually the relationship type—would she want that from him?

From Eli's experience, finding a man was like buying a car to some women. There were those who were constantly searching for a fast ride and willing to test-drive anything that got them to sixty the fastest. Then, there were those who took their time and compared features and quality before committing to it. And then there were women, like Annalise and Trudie, who preferred to take cabs.

He got the sense that Lucy was a cab rider, the kind of woman who didn't need a man to be happy and didn't waste a lot of time and energy searching. But it really didn't make a difference. A few kisses now and then didn't mean they were in a relationship.

He should be happy that she wasn't demanding more of him. So why did he want to give her everything she'd never ask for?

He glanced over at her. "What are you going to do if you get lost?" he asked.

"How could I get lost? I'm not going to wander around out here by myself. If I can't see the cabin, then I don't go there."

"I used to think that, too. Until I got lost and spent a night out here by myself."

"What happened?"

"I was spending the summer with my grandmother and we had a fight about something. So I decided to take off, just for a quick walk. But I got turned around. Just like that. One second I knew where I was and the next I didn't. So my next piece of advice is to always carry a compass. And spend some time studying the landmarks."

Over the next hour, Eli gave her a lesson in navigating the wilderness. He tried to impress on her the dangers that she faced if she wasn't careful, but Lucy assured him that she wasn't planning to take any long walks, no matter what the cause.

By the end of his lesson, she was clearly over-loaded with information and had begun to tune him out, just smiling and nodding at everything he told her. He'd have to stop for now. As he steered them through the woods and back to the meadow, he reached out to take her hand, helping her over rough parts of the trail. It was enough just to touch her, to feel that momentary connection when her hand was tucked into his.

When they arrived at the cabin, Eli stayed on the porch while she went inside to make lunch. But to his surprise, she opened the screen door a few moments later and invited him in.

"It's not against the guidelines anymore for me to come inside?"

"It's your cabin."

He hesitated before walking in the front door. Eli was used to the cabin the way his grandmother had left it and he wondered if she'd done anything to alter the interior. But as he stepped inside, he noticed that everything was in its proper place, almost as if Lucy had treated the cabin like a shrine.

"I love this place," he murmured.

"Me, too. I mean, I know it's not mine, but I can feel your grandmother's presence here. And I think she approves. And that's important to me."

"Why don't you sit down and let me make you breakfast for lunch. I'm a pretty decent cook. And I used to make it for Trudie all the time."

"I don't have real eggs," she said. "Just the powdered kind. And powdered milk."

"That'll do for pancakes," he said.

She sat down at the table and watched him for

a long moment, then picked up a small video camera and aimed it at him. "So what is it you do with yourself when you're not trudging up mountains with caramel lattes and making buckwheat pancakes, Eli Montgomery?"

"You're not really filming me, are you?"

"Yes, I am. But this is for my personal use."

He chuckled softly. "Then wait a moment." He reached for the hem of his T-shirt then pulled it up over his head, revealing his naked chest. "How's that?"

"Fine," she said. "Flex, please."

"I don't really have a regular job," Eli continued. "I bounce from place to place. The last six months I've been in Nicaragua surveying the site for a new canal that a Chinese billionaire hopes to build. Before that, I was on a trekking expedition in Mongolia. I've traveled the world by freighter. An opportunity pops up and off I go."

"And what's your next job?"

"I don't know," Eli said. "I'm waiting to see what comes along."

He mixed the batter for the pancakes and then stirred in some dried blueberries. When he found his grandmother's favorite cast-iron skillet, Eli set it on the stove and added some oil.

"Did Trudie teach you to cook?" she asked.

"A little. Buck, my grandfather, makes great food. I spent a lot of time with him while my mom was gone on expeditions."

The scent of pancakes filled the cabin and brought Riley in. He sat down right next to the stove. Eli flipped a pancake to the dog, then stacked the rest on a plate for Lucy. He found a tin of maple syrup on a shelf above the stove and set it down beside her plate, then leaned close and brushed a kiss across her lips. "Enjoy," he murmured.

"I do," Lucy said, her gaze fixed on his.

He sat down across from her and crossed his arms over his chest.

"You're not going to eat?"

"I'd rather watch you," he murmured.

She poured some syrup over the pancakes and dug in.

"Good?" he asked.

"Mmm. So good. I miss fresh food so much. I started digging a garden, but it's going to be forever until I actually have vegetables. We had frost just a couple days ago."

"Plant cold weather crops first. Lettuce, radishes, carrots, beets. That's what my grandmother did."

"More advice," she said. She cut a bit of her pancake and held it out to him. "Eat."

He smiled and swallowed. "Maybe I am hungry."

Lucy pushed away from the table and took the chair next to him, then handed him her fork. As he ate, she scooped up some syrup with her finger and licked it off with her tongue.

Eli stopped chewing, stunned at the erotic undertones of her action. He didn't believe she'd done it deliberately, but being so close to her was having a powerful effect on his body. She did it again and he reached out and gently grabbed her wrist.

"Stop doing that."

Lucy frowned. "Why?"

"Just stop."

Tipping her chin up, she scooped up more of the syrup and licked her finger again, then slowly realized why he'd stopped her. "Oh," she murmured.

"You do it again, I may have to kiss you."

She grinned, then wiped her finger on the plate one last time. But she didn't put her finger in her mouth. Instead, she wiped the syrup on her bottom lip. Leaning across the table, she smiled at him in a silent invitation.

Groaning, he put down his fork and accepted her challenge, kissing her softly, lingering over her mouth.

He slowly stood and pulled her to her feet, then smoothed his hands over her waist. Pressing her back against the edge of the table, he deepened the kiss, his tongue invading the sweet warmth of her mouth.

Lucy reached back and brushed her plate aside and it clattered to the floor. Riley ran over and gobbled down the pancakes.

"Don't worry, I'll make you more," he murmured, and bent to take her lips again.

Lucy was breathless, her thoughts spinning inside her head, making her dizzy with desire. She wasn't sure whether to stop him, or to grab his broad, naked shoulders and pull him down onto the table. This was supposed to be wrong but it felt so wonderful that she didn't want him to stop.

His chest was smooth and rippled with muscles and her fingers danced over the tanned skin, the nerves alive with excitement. He was so strong and sure of himself that she hadn't thought to deny him—

or herself. But as they arched against each other, Lucy realized where they were heading.

She'd invested so much in this cabin experience and it was meant to be about solitude and introspection. Now, she was putting the entire project at risk. How was she supposed to spend the next month focused on the tasks at hand when all she wanted to do was seduce Eli Montgomery?

"Stop," she murmured, gently pushing against his chest.

He drew back and stared down into her eyes. It only took a few seconds for him to see the determination in her request and he stepped away. "Sorry," he said.

"No, don't apologize. It's my fault. I started it with the syrup. I shouldn't complicate things. I have a job to do here and you are a very dangerous distraction."

He chuckled softly. "And I'm against the rules."

"Well, yes. That's a big part of the problem. I'm supposed to be alone. Except for one day a month."

"Trudie had lots of male visitors. She was known for her...hospitality."

"And so you think I should sleep with any man who wanders by?"

"No! Of course not. I'm just saying that it's only normal to have desires, especially when you're so isolated like this. And Trudie did."

Lucy shook her head. "No. I'm not going to put this project at risk just because you're hot and I can't keep my hands off of you. All I need is for the media to find out what was happening up here and it would turn a serious show into a joke." Lucy pushed against his chest and slipped out of his embrace. "No, no. I don't want anything from you. You need to leave and I have to stop acting like some love-starved fool."

Eli reached out and smoothed her tumbled hair out of her face. "You're not a fool. If you are, then so am I. Do you think I expected this? I expected to hate you. I was angry at Annalise for renting you the cabin. I was angry at you for taking advantage of my grandmother's memory and putting yourself in danger. I wanted you gone. And then I met you."

"This is all Annalise's fault. If she wouldn't have sent you, we never would have met each other."

He took another step back and she fought the urge to reach out and grab him. In her entire life, she'd never experienced this kind of desire for a man. But there were choices to be made. "It would be best for you to go," Lucy said. "And don't return."

Eli nodded. "So, I guess I'll see you in ten months," he murmured.

Lucy groaned inwardly. A month seemed like a year. Ten months was going to seem like…ten years. How could she have been so stupid? She should have stopped this before it even started. "I guess so," Lucy said.

There. She'd made a decision and she was going to stick to it. She'd stop fantasizing about Eli Montgomery—she'd put the man completely out of her mind and get on with the business of producing a great show.

"Come on," she said. "I'll walk you as far as the meadow."

Eli grabbed his T-shirt and tugged it over his head, then moved toward the door. Riley trailed after him, hoping for another blueberry pancake. Lucy followed them both out. As he pulled his empty pack over his shoulder, she grabbed his gun and held it out to him.

"I want you to know that I admire you for what you're trying to do out here," Eli said, as they headed for the meadow.

She glanced over at him, emotion swelling inside of her. She didn't want him to leave. It wasn't even noon yet. But Lucy had to keep telling herself that she was doing the right thing. "Thank you," she said.

He slipped his arm around her shoulders and they walked on in silence. When they reached the edge of the meadow, he bent close and pressed a kiss to her cheek. "Good luck, Lucy. And stay safe."

She felt tears gathering at the corners of her eyes, but Lucy refused to surrender. Instead, she pasted a bright smile on her face and watched as he trudged back through the meadow, leaving her for the second time. But this time was different. There was no anticipation of his return. Only a deep and painful loneliness that seem to settle around her heart. She bent down and gave Riley a pat on the head. "It's for the best," she said to the dog.

He didn't look back when he got to the trailhead. There was no last wave or indication that he knew she was watching. And when he disappeared into the trees, Lucy let out a tightly held breath.

She'd plant her garden and build her cabin. She'd learn to pickle vegetables and forage for herbal remedies. And she'd do it all without thinking of Eli Montgomery. From now on, he was banished from her mind.

Lucy turned to walk back to the cabin, but then froze. A huge dark shadow moved along the length of the porch and she reached down to grab Riley's collar before he noticed the bear. Just as she was closing her fingers around the nylon of his collar, the dog bolted and took off toward the cabin at a full run.

"Riley, no!" she shouted. "Stop. Riley. Come here."

Her heart slammed in her chest and she ran as fast as she could, but it was no use. The dog reached the cabin long before she did. Lucy stopped a distance away, watching in horror as Riley barked and growled at the intruder. At first, the bear seemed confused, but then it lumbered off the porch and started toward the dog.

Lucy put her arms up, screaming and shouting, hoping that between the two of them, they could frighten it off. When it started toward her, she frantically tried to remember the advice Eli had given her. This was a black bear, not a grizzly, so scaring him was the best option.

She pulled her shirttail up behind her, trying to make herself as big as she could, then drew a deep breath and roared in a low and menacing voice. Suddenly, to her relief, the bear turned and ran off, disappearing into the woods on the far side of the cabin.

Riley followed him for a distance, while Lucy raced to the cabin. She hurried inside and slammed the screen door, then called frantically for Riley. When he appeared on the porch, she pulled him inside and shoved the plank door closed.

Breathless and terrified, she stood in the middle of the cabin, her body trembling. She'd thought that Eli was the biggest danger she'd face out here. But there were plenty of other things that could take her out. She'd just met one of them.

Lucy plopped down on the floor and buried her face in her hands. She'd never felt more vulnerable in her life. And it had only taken ten measly minutes for her to regret sending Eli away.

3

July

"WHAT DO YOU have growing here?"

Lucy pushed to her feet and walked over to where Eli stood. "Beans," she said. "Something keeps eating them, though."

"Probably rabbits," he said. "My grandmother used to put up a wire fence to keep them out. I think the posts and wire are still stored underneath the cabin. I could set it up for you, if you'd like."

"I'll put it up if you could get it for me," Lucy suggested.

He nodded, then turned and headed toward the rear of the cabin. Lucy watched him, closing her eyes and drawing a deep breath. After what had happened in June, she'd assumed that he'd send Annalise this month. But he'd made excuses for her again and Lucy was left to wonder if he'd even asked her to take his place.

She should have sent him away, but she'd been hit with such a confusing combo of happiness and anger at his presence that she'd instead just showed him her vegetable garden.

Was he deliberately tempting her? She couldn't believe that he'd use his seductive powers for malicious purposes. She didn't know him well, but she was sure she could trust him to have her best interests at heart. After all, every visit included a lengthy safety lecture and demonstration.

The only other explanation was that he found her so overwhelmingly attractive he just couldn't help himself. And Lucy figured that was a long shot at best. Perhaps the only way to know for sure was to ask him.

When he reappeared from around the cabin, he carried a roll of wire and some short, metal fence stakes. He set them at the edge of her garden, then walked over to stand next to her. "If you need help with the fence, I can—"

"Why did you come, Eli? Did you even ask Annalise to make the trip? Tell me the truth." She glanced over at him and bit back a groan. He'd tossed his T-shirt aside earlier and now a thin sheen of sweat covered his tan shoulders and torso. He was simply the most beautiful man she'd ever met, and that certainly didn't help matters.

"I told you, she was busy. I didn't want to come. I didn't want to make things more difficult for you." He bent down and began to pull weeds from around her beets, the muscles rippling across his back as he moved.

There had been other men in her life, but they'd been very simple and short affairs. And though she'd always felt an initial physical attraction, it was never long before the heat faded and the fire died out.

Lucy had to wonder if that might happen with Eli. Though they'd made a few tentative steps toward seduction, they'd both had the sense to stop before they went too far. But Lucy couldn't get past the feeling that he wanted more—even if she didn't.

"Can you just leave the weeds," she said. "I'll get to them later."

He shook his head as he chuckled. "Come on, Lucy. I can pull a few weeds in your garden, can't I? I understand you're supposed to do everything on your own, but now you're getting a bit obsessive, don't you think?"

She'd been holding her temper since he'd arrived and now he was handing her an argument on a silver platter. Lucy clenched her jaw and fought the urge to snap at him. Maybe that's what it would take for him to understand how confused she felt.

"It looks like rain," she said, pointing to some dark clouds on the western horizon. "You might want to get going."

Eli slowly straightened, tossing a handful of weeds out into the meadow. "Are you all right? You seem a bit tense."

"No, I'm fine." Lucy sucked in a sharp breath. "No, that's not true. I'm not fine at all. I'm—I'm—"

"Angry?"

"Yes!"

"Frustrated?"

"Yes!"

He carefully crossed the rows of vegetables to stand in front of her. "Would you like to explain what's wrong?"

Lucy gathered her resolve. Though it went against

every self-preserving instinct she had, she knew her decision was for the best. "I don't think you even asked Annalise to come this month. I was quite clear that I didn't want you to come and yet you ignored my wishes. Everything is so complicated when you're here."

Eli glanced around. "This is complicated? We're pulling a few weeds in your garden."

"I know. But tell me your mind's not on something else. Tell me you don't want to kiss me. Right here, right now."

"And what if I did? I've kissed you before and you haven't objected. You even seemed to enjoy it."

She watched as his gaze lazily skimmed over her features. But when he reached out and made as if to slip his hand around her waist, Lucy avoided his touch. "If we can't keep this on a strictly professional level, then it's best if someone else does these monthly check-ins. If your mother can't come, then I'll ask the producers to find someone else."

"Fine," Eli said. "That's a good idea."

"Great." Lucy took a deep breath and nodded. Now that she'd cleared up that one important matter, she expected to feel a bit of relief. But instead, a deep sense of loneliness set in. Without his visits to look forward to, the rest of her time on the mountain seemed to stretch out in front of her like a long, gray road.

"Now will you explain what this is really about," Eli said. "And if you bring up those damn guidelines, I swear, I will tear that cabin apart until I find those rules and set them on fire."

She turned away from him and walked to the other

side of the garden. "When you're not here, I think about you."

"I think about you, too. What's wrong with that?"

"I think about you *a lot*. And not just about what we do. I imagine what we could be doing. In bed. On the couch. On the floor by the fire. In the meadow. It's become a distraction."

Eli slowly stepped closer. "We're attracted to each other. It's not like we're the first two people on the planet who've experienced sexual attraction." He reached out and grabbed her hand and gently turned her to face him. "It's all pretty simple, really."

Lucy bent down to pick up an old ceramic bowl, then walked over to the row of lettuce that she'd planted. Squatting down, she began to tear leaves from the plants and drop them into the bowl. "I've always been quite happy on my own. I like being in charge of my life. And I've never, ever felt lonely." She glanced over her shoulder at him. "Until now."

"Well, of course you do. You're stuck out here all by yourself. They don't let you use a phone or your computer and I'm the only person—"

"No, you don't understand. I never get lonely. Ever. And—and I don't like how it makes me feel."

"How?"

"Weak. Silly. Angry. I need to be able to do this by myself, without any help. Without any distractions."

He held his hand out and pulled her up, his fingers splaying around her waist.

"So, that's what you think I am?"

She looked up at him and nodded. "A big distraction."

Eli bent forward and brushed a kiss across her

mouth. Lucy bit back a moan and tried to keep her knees from buckling beneath her.

If she had to say goodbye to him today, she wanted one last memory. Just one kiss, that's all she'd allow.

"Stop," she said.

He bent closer, but this time, the kiss lasted a bit longer, his tongue teasing at the crease in her mouth. He slid his palms beneath the hem of her shirt and when he reached her waist, he splayed his fingers on her skin. The contact sent a shiver of anticipation up her spine.

Lucy couldn't help herself. She wanted more and she didn't want him to stop at all. Her palms slid across his chest, tracing a path over the smooth flesh and hard muscle. He really was perfect, flawless, the kind of man that no woman could resist.

Why did she think she was special? She had the same desires as any other woman, the same hormones racing through her body. The same need to experience pleasure. She moaned softly as his hand drifted along her ribs before cupping her naked breast beneath the soft fabric of her T-shirt.

Her heart slammed against the inside of her chest and she felt light-headed and completely out of control. Her ability to resist him was nonexistent and Lucy wondered if she'd only imagined it was there in the first place. Was this it? Was surrender her only option?

"Stop," she murmured again.

He slowly drew back then met her gaze. Lucy gasped for breath, trying to clear her head and form a rational thought. "You have to go. Now. Right away."

"Lucy, this is crazy. Do you really think that if you—"

She pressed her fingertips to his lips. "I said you need to leave. Please don't argue with me."

With that, she spun around and ran to the cabin, slipping inside and slamming the thick plank door behind her.

A soft knock sounded at the door. "Lucy?"

"Go away," she shouted.

"Just promise me something."

"What?"

"Promise me that you'll watch out for yourself. That you'll be safe. And that if you need help, you'll call me."

She took a ragged breath, leaning forward to press her forehead against the door. "I will. I promise." Lucy listened to his footsteps on the porch, heard him pick up his pack and slip it over his shoulders. A few minutes later, there was no sound and she opened the door a crack and looked out.

He was already halfway across the meadow, his stride long and relaxed. Eli didn't glance over his shoulder this time. When he got to the tree line, he just disappeared. Forever.

Lucy drew a deep breath and let it out slowly, waiting for the flood of relief to come over her. But after a second breath, the only thing she felt was a deep and empty loneliness. This time, he wouldn't be back.

"WHAT ARE YOU doing here? Was I expecting you?"

Eli looked up from his empty glass of whiskey to see his mother standing in her kitchen doorway. She was wearing a sparkly dress that was a bit too short for his tastes. "I hiked up to the cabin today," he murmured. "I thought I'd stop by for a chat."

Annalise wandered over to the cupboard and grabbed a tumbler, then filled it with ice from the freezer. After pouring herself a whiskey, she sat down across from Eli. "I don't know why I bother with men," she said. "They're more trouble than they're worth."

"You and Mr. Wonderful having problems?" Eli asked.

"He can be such an ass. I can't believe I was actually considering marrying him."

Eli reached for the whiskey and poured a bit into his empty glass. "Are you happy, Mom? You always seem as if you're searching for something more. Do you think you'll ever find it?"

"I don't know. I guess I have...what do they call it...that problem where I can't focus on one thing for a long time?"

"Attention deficit disorder?"

"Hmm. Yeah." She took a sip of the whiskey. "What about you?"

"I'm not sure. Things might be changing. I'm thinking about making some plans for myself."

Annalise stared at him for a long moment. "What? Have you been seeing someone?"

"Yeah. Kind of. It's still early, but she's...she's different. I like her. More than anyone else I've ever met. We just get along. And she understands me."

"That's important," Annalise said. "I don't think anyone has ever really gotten me. Except, maybe—"

"Who?"

"Your father," she said. "He seemed to know exactly who I was."

"You never talk about him."

Annalise shook her head. "You told me you didn't want to hear it."

"When did I say that?"

She considered the question for a long moment. "I think you were sixteen and we were arguing about your plans for college and I brought him up and you—"

"I assumed you didn't want to talk about him," Eli said.

"I thought you hated him," Annalise said.

"I never met him. How could I hate him?"

She drew a deep breath and then let it out slowly. "I had a visitor while you were gone this winter." Pushing to her feet, she crossed to the kitchen and pulled a large envelope from the mess on her desk. Silently, she set it in front of him.

"What is this?" he asked, examining the envelope.

"It's… It's from your father's family. His oldest son, Malcolm Quinn. A few months ago, they had an expedition to Everest and they found your father's body. He had a journal and he wrote in it right before he died. He mentioned you."

"They know about me?"

Annalise nodded. "Yes. And they'd like to meet you sometime."

Eli sat back in his chair and raked his hands through his hair, at a complete loss for words. There had been moments in his life when he'd wondered about his father, wondered what kind of man he was. All Annalise had told him was that Max Quinn had died on Everest and had been married with a family, and Eli hadn't wanted to learn anything more.

The less he knew, the easier it was to forget about Max Quinn.

But now, there was contact, a brother, people who had lived with the man and known him well. Was he really ready to open that door? "Malcolm?"

"Yes. He's the oldest. Then there are twins, they're a year older than you are. Ryan and Rogan. And the youngest is a girl. Dana."

"I have four siblings," he said.

"Half siblings," she said. Annalise cleared her throat. "There's something else, as well." She reached for the envelope and pulled out a sheaf of papers. "Since you're the son of Max Quinn, then you're also in line for an inheritance from Max's great-aunt, Aileen Quinn."

Eli chuckled softly. "Siblings and an inheritance. All in one night. I'm a lucky guy."

"You are. The inheritance is almost a million dollars."

Eli stared at his mother, certain that he'd imagined the words she'd just said. "Very funny. What am I really getting? Some silver teapot? Salt and pepper shakers?"

"No, it's really a million dollars. Your great-great-aunt is Aileen Quinn, the very famous Irish novelist. She's a multimillionaire and she's giving away her money to the direct descendants of her four brothers." She pointed to the papers. "It's all there. You just need to take a DNA test to prove you're a Quinn."

Eli scanned the words on the paper, but they all seemed to meld into a giant blur. What the hell was happening here? He'd sat down at the table with a bottle of whiskey to contemplate his future with Lucy

Parker. And now, just an hour later, he had four siblings, a great-great-aunt and a boatload of money. "Why didn't you tell me this earlier? I've been home for three months."

"I wanted to wait for the right moment."

He glanced over at her and saw the look of distress on her face. "What? There's something else?"

Annalise nodded. "And before I say anything, you have to understand that I've always wanted to protect you and to make things easier for you."

"What?" Eli asked.

"The DNA test. It may or may not prove that you're Max Quinn's son."

The news hit him like a slap to the face. Though he hadn't spent a lot of time thinking about his father, he had assumed that Annalise had been telling the truth all along.

"It was just one night. He was a climber with another expedition, and once I took up with Max, it was over. And considering the number of nights I was with Max...well, the odds were definitely in his favor."

Eli shoved the chair away from the table and stood. "I gotta get out of here."

"Darling, please don't be angry with me. I've just tried to do what was best. I really believe Max is your father. You look like him. You look like your brothers."

Eli shook his head. He could forgive his mother for a lot of things, but she'd never lied to him. And now, this whole fairy tale of his fatherhood might be a complete fabrication. For all he knew, his father was still alive and completely unaware of his existence.

He glanced down at the papers that were clutched

in his hand. He wanted to burn them, to forget any of this had ever happened. What did he need it for? He knew exactly who he was. Would a million dollars and a few siblings change that?

Eli strode to the back porch and grabbed his pack, shoving the papers inside.

"Where are you going?"

"I have no idea," he said.

"Please, don't leave. Let's just talk about this. I don't want you to be angry with me."

"I'm not," Eli said. "You're right. You were just trying to protect me." He paused and cursed beneath his breath. "But there are times, Annalise, when I wish you'd just get your damn act together and at least pretend to be the parent in this relationship."

He slipped his pack onto his shoulders and jogged down the front steps. Eli wasn't sure where he was going, but he couldn't stay here any longer. There were too many things to sort through in his head and it would be impossible to do with Annalise hovering over him, trying to plead her case.

As he jogged out to his truck, his mother watched him from the front door of her bungalow. "I love you," she shouted. "Please don't forget that."

There were plenty of places he could go to lose himself, favorite spots that he and Buck had explored over the years. But he steered the truck out of town, in the direction of the trailhead that would lead him to his grandmother's cabin. It felt right to go there, to be with Lucy, to find out what she thought of everything that was happening in his life.

Cursing softly, Eli pulled over to the side of the road. When had she become so important to him?

Lately, he couldn't go an hour, much less a day, without thinking about her. And now, when his life had suddenly turned into a chaotic mess, she was the only person he wanted to see.

Hell, he should be able to handle this on his own. Life's little problems had never confounded him in the past. But there was comfort in knowing that Lucy would listen and tell him what was simple and true. She had an uncanny way of cutting through all the crap and getting right to the heart of the matter.

Still, after their disagreement earlier that day, Eli wasn't sure she'd welcome him back. He understood her need to maintain her independence, but was she really intent on driving him away? Or was there something else at work?

In just a very short time, they'd formed a unique friendship. More than a friendship, a romance. And though it didn't follow the normal course that most romances did, it was still something that continued to intrigue him. He didn't want to put it aside simply because Lucy had some misgivings or fears that she couldn't articulate.

She might insist she didn't need him, not in the traditional sense, but right now, he needed her. And though he was treading in very unfamiliar territory, without even a map or a compass to guide him, Eli had to follow his instincts. Right now, those instincts were leading him back to the mountain.

SHE'D SLEPT IN that morning, her naked body curled beneath the soft, faded quilt, her face buried in the down pillows. Though she'd looked forward to Eli's visit, the aftermath was almost too much to bear.

Groaning, she reached for the video camera on the bedside table and flipped open the screen. She found the footage she'd taken yesterday in her garden and replayed it, her gaze focused on Eli. He'd discarded his shirt and wore just his hiking shorts and his boots. A shiver skittered down her spine as she paused the video to take a closer examination of his chest and belly.

"God," she murmured. It might be a lot easier to put her feelings aside if the sight of his body didn't send her into paroxysms of desire. Her fingers twitched as she remembered the feel of his bare skin beneath her hands.

Searching for something to distract herself, Lucy tossed the camera aside and crawled out of bed, grabbing an old T-shirt to pull over herself. Riley lifted his head from the other pillow, then yawned and went back to sleep.

Rubbing her eyes, she crossed the room and set the teakettle on the woodstove then opened the front door and carefully rebuilt the fire. Then she put some granola into a bowl and mixed some powdered milk and water to pour over it. As she ate, Lucy went over her list of tasks for the day. She was two logs behind on the cabin, she still had more of the garden to dig up and she needed to erect a rabbit fence.

By the time she was finished eating, the teakettle was boiling. She made herself a cup of coffee, added powdered creamer and sugar, then opened the front door and stared out at the morning sky. Exhaustion seemed to drag her down with every step and she sighed in frustration. She'd been hoping for rain, but the sky was clear.

This was exactly what she didn't want. She'd spent the entire night tossing and turning and thinking about the last words she'd said to Eli and now she was too tired to work.

It really hadn't been fair to burden him with all her insecurities. He'd walked away as confused as she was. But she was quickly reaching a point of no return with him and she had to do what was right for this project.

He'd become too important to her. She spent too many hours daydreaming about him, wondering what he was doing when they were apart. She couldn't count the number of times she'd wondered how to get ahold of him, aching to hear his voice for just a minute or two. The computer had become a looming temptation and, had she known his email address, she might have given in.

But loneliness was a sign of weakness. She'd lived almost her entire life by relying solely on her own wits and resources. She'd had parents once, and then foster parents, but they'd given her so little that she'd learned to expect nothing from other human beings.

Only now Eli had walked into her life. And in just a few short encounters, he'd managed to make her want more. She used to revel in her solitude but now all she could think about was having him here with her. As a friend and a companion. Maybe even a lover. One day a month just wasn't enough.

She understood why she was so attracted to him. He was sexy and charming, of course, but it ran deeper than that. There was an intellectual connection as well. He understood what she was trying to accomplish here; he got that it wasn't just some reality TV show, it was deeply personal to her. She'd never felt that kind of understanding and acceptance with anyone before.

She wasn't an easy person to get along with, she didn't trust people enough to make good friends. But with Eli, the walls just seemed to disappear. There was an ease to their conversations that she found comforting. They'd enjoyed the same books and laughed at the same jokes. They were both a bit cynical yet secretly optimistic.

There was also the physical aspect. She couldn't deny the way he made her feel when he touched her or kissed her. And in the hours before she fell asleep, the desire she'd been trying to bury all day long would surface and she would construct wild sexual fantasies about the two of them, fantasies that sometimes made her blush.

But the most startling thing that she'd found in Eli was an emotional connection. He made her feel safe and confident. She knew that at least one person in the world cared about her. And when he was near, Lucy was genuinely happy.

And yet, even with all this to offer, she'd made a deal, and a promise to herself that she'd see this project out to the end. It had seemed simple when she'd signed the contract. And the last thing she'd expected was a handsome, sexy man walking into her life and turning it upside down.

With a soft sigh, Lucy stared out the screen door, her gaze fixed on the meadow. A warm breeze skimmed over her bare legs and she drew a deep breath. She'd get back on track today. There was plenty of work to do in her garden and she still had logs to cut for her cabin.

Riley nudged at the door and she let him out. The dog took off down the steps and a few seconds later began barking. "Riley!" she called, stepping out on the porch.

She stopped short when she saw the tent, set up just below the steps. A few seconds later, the flap opened and Eli crawled out, rubbing his eyes against the morning sun. Lucy stared at him, wondering what could have possibly brought him back to the cabin. But then he smiled at her and she realized she didn't really care. He was here and she was happy again.

With a soft cry, she ran down the steps and threw herself into his arms. His mouth came down on hers, fast and desperate, his tongue slipping between her lips and tasting deeply.

She'd never felt this way before, so wild and un-inhibited. She stopped thinking rationally and operated on pure instinct. Her hands tangled in his hair, her legs wrapped tightly around his waist, her body arched against his until she wasn't sure where she ended and he began.

"Tell me what you want," he said, his breath warm against her ear. "Say it."

"I want you," Lucy replied, tipping her head back so that his lips could taste the curve of her neck. Her pulse raced and her breath came in short gasps and when he carried her over to the porch and set her down, she sighed softly, pulling him along with her.

She thought at first he was wearing shorts, but then realized he was dressed only in his boxers, the thin cotton fabric providing little barrier to his growing erection. With a smile, she rubbed her hips against his, causing a groan to slip from deep in his throat.

"Are you all right here?" he asked.

She nodded. "Fine."

"I don't want you to get...splinters."

His concern, though sweet, seemed at that moment to be completely ridiculous and Lucy began to giggle. He drew back and looked down at her. "Sorry," she said.

"Splinters could be a problem."

"I guess they could. But then, there are also the bears. We could be attacked while we're, you know, in the midst of it all."

"And there are the snakes. You've got to watch out for rattlesnakes."

"Mountain lions," she said.

"We could get struck by lightning."

"Would you like to go inside?" she asked.

"Isn't that against the guidelines?"

"To hell with the guidelines," she muttered.

He grinned and shook his head. "I think we'll be just fine right here. But I do need to take care of one thing." He pushed away from the step and walked over to his tent. A few seconds later, he returned with a small plastic packet.

"You came prepared?"

"I keep a supply in my bag," he said. "Just in case."

"A good rifle, a comfortable pair of hiking boots and a supply of condoms. What every man should pack before heading out on the trail."

He braced his hands on either side of her head and leaned into her, his body brushing hers in a provocative way. "Are we going to spend all our time talking or should I kiss you again?"

"Kiss me," she said.

He pulled her on top of him, settling her legs on either side of his hips before he began a slow, lazy exploration of her body. Her T-shirt came off after only a few moments and the feel of the summer breeze on her naked body made every sensation more intense.

Eli drew her closer, nuzzling her breast before teasing at the nipple with his tongue. Lucy wondered why she'd been so afraid of this, so determined to push him away. There was nothing wrong with enjoying the physical attraction between them.

He shifted, his hard shaft pressing against the damp spot between her thighs. Suddenly, she couldn't wait any longer. There was no need for seduction. Lucy knew exactly what she wanted and she was determined to have it.

She reached down and hooked her fingers around the waistband of his boxers, then slowly drew them down along his hips. When he kicked them aside, she found the condom and tore open the packet.

Eli closed his eyes as she smoothed the latex over his shaft. A moment later, she moved above him until his erection pressed at her warm entrance. Grasping her hips, Eli gently guided her down on top of him, drawing her closer until he was buried deep inside her.

As she began to move, Lucy realized this was more than just a physical attraction. She'd never experienced anything so perfect, so right. Eli was sweet and sexy, but he was also a man who accepted her exactly the way she was.

The pleasure began to build deep inside her, but this time, she wasn't afraid to let go. With Eli, she didn't feel vulnerable. She didn't want to hide her emotions. She wanted him to see her surrender, to know that he was giving her what other men hadn't.

Lucy pressed her hands against his chest and tipped her head back, pleasure pulsing through her body with each stroke. But when Eli reached between them and touched her, she was lost. Every nerve in her body tingled, every ounce of her attention was focused on the spot where they were joined.

And then it hit her, powerful spasms that rocked her body, coursing through her like an electrical current and leaving her skin flushed and her nerves tingling. Somewhere in the midst of her release, he'd joined her, and as Lucy drifted down to reality, she opened her eyes and watched Eli do the same.

Lucy collapsed against his chest. "Why did you come back to me?" she asked.

"I just wanted to talk to you. I needed to hear your voice."

"That's it?"

"No, but the rest can wait," he said.

"Tell me," Lucy insisted.

"Well, I just found out that I may or may not have inherited a million dollars. And that the man I thought was my father maybe isn't my father at all, and my real father could actually be alive."

Lucy frowned. "You could just admit you missed me."

"All right. I missed you. And there was no way I wanted to leave things the way we did yesterday."

She laughed. "A millionaire?"

"It's a very long and complicated story and I'll explain it later."

She leaned closer and dropped a kiss on his lips. "I want to hear all about it."

They spent the entire day together and never put all of their clothes back on. After a morning in bed, they spread a blanket in the grass in front of the cabin, and had a picnic lunch. Then they planted a few more rows of vegetables in her garden before returning to the bed for a nap.

But a day was all she'd allow herself. The project had to come first.

So he left that night. She kissed him goodbye and made him promise that he'd return in a month. As he walked away, four weeks apart seemed an impossible thought to Lucy. And yet, it had to be her reality, at least until next April.

4

August

THE CALL HAD come at 3:00 a.m. Annalise drove over from her house and woke Eli from a deep and dreamless sleep. Lucy Parker had missed her weekly check-in with the producers and they were worried something had happened to her.

In less than five minutes, Eli had thrown together a pack and was ready to leave. With a light load, he could get to the cabin in under three hours. The rescue helicopter could get there faster, but Eli knew from being on the team that they wouldn't be able to take off until dawn, and Eli couldn't sit around and wait until then. He had to go now.

He grabbed his satellite phone on the way out, aware that he was also taking a risk by hiking the trail in the dark. But he'd made the trip so often, Eli was sure he could do it, even with his eyes closed. A flashlight made the trip almost easy.

With his rifle slung over his shoulder, Eli kept a close watch on the trail for bears or other hazards, making as much noise as he could. But in his mind, his only thought was Lucy, and he couldn't help but run back through his last trip to the mountain cabin. They'd grown so close in such a short amount of time and it had been almost impossible to leave her.

But he knew how important the project was to Lucy and he'd decided to let her call the shots. This thing between him and Lucy Parker was still in a very hazy, undefined state. It wasn't exactly a relationship, and yet he found himself caught up in fantasies about the future all the time. In truth, the past month, his mind had been filled with thoughts of the few hours that they'd spent together.

He ought to have moved on to his next adventure already. Instead, he'd worked in his mother's shop, caught up on his reading and signed up for a weekly shift with the local search-and-rescue unit. As much as Eli wanted to deny it, he was turning into a damn homebody, and all because he wanted to hang around just one more month.

He glanced at his watch. The sun would be up in a half hour, but he was nearly to the meadow. Though he wasn't sure what he'd find, all sorts of scenarios raced through his head at once. He'd been concerned from the beginning that Lucy was in over her head. He'd been impressed by her determination and grit, so he'd stepped back from his self-imposed protector role. But now he kicked himself for letting down his guard. She could be injured, lying helpless somewhere near the cabin. There could have been a bear attack or she could have simply fallen and hit her head.

Eli had come to think of her as stubbornly invincible. But he should have known that image was pure fantasy. Out here, in the wild, everyone was vulnerable. Everyone was just one step away from disaster.

He tried to focus on something more positive to keep himself from panicking, and his mind wandered to the morning they'd made love. He'd relived that moment again and again over the past three weeks, patiently waiting for the next visit. He would be patient no longer.

Thunder rumbled in the distance and Eli squinted through the trees at the eastern sky. A storm was rolling in over the Rockies, and the conditions could change very quickly. If she was outside— No, he wasn't going to dwell on the worst-case scenarios.

Maybe her radio had broken, or the generator had run out of gas. There were so many benign events that could have caused her to miss the call. Hell, maybe she'd just lost track of time and forgot.

As he reached the meadow, Eli grabbed his water bottle and took a long drink. Then, after tucking it back in the pocket, he took off running, the way to the cabin now visible in the low light of dawn.

The rain began suddenly, a downpour that nearly obliterated his view. The cool water washed away the dust and sweat from the trail and gave him fresh energy—energy he'd need if he found Lucy hurt.

The smell of fresh, clean air filled his head, reminding him of his boyhood and the summers spent on the mountain. Life had been so uncomplicated then; choices had been simple. He'd made sure to keep his life that way, even into adulthood. He'd never really committed to anything, never made a hard choice, never learned what sacrifice or compromise was.

Hell, for the past ten years, he'd wandered from adventure to adventure, searching for that one thing that might catch his attention, that piqued his passion. Wouldn't it be the ultimate irony if he'd found that here, on Trudie's mountain? If he found it with Lucy?

"Hello!" he called as he approached the cabin. "Lucy?"

A few seconds later, the cabin door opened a crack and Riley peeked out. But he didn't approach Eli. Instead, he sat behind the screen door, watching and waiting, his tail beating on the rough plank floor.

"Hey, buddy," Eli said as he climbed the porch steps. He opened the door and patted the dog's head as he stepped inside. Eli stopped short as he took in the mess that was the interior.

"Lucy?" It was not like her to leave everything in such a state. A flare of panic gripped him. If she wasn't here, he had no idea where to look.

Riley ran over to the far side of the bed and whined softly. Eli crossed the room and was stunned by the scene in front of him. Lucy was curled up on the rough plank floor, a quilt wrapped around her naked body, her hair damp and tangled.

Eli squatted down. "Lucy?" He gently shook her shoulder and her eyes fluttered open.

At first she didn't seem to recognize him. Then she reached out and touched his cheek. "Hi. You're here."

"I am."

"Is it really you?"

"What are you doing on the floor?"

She frowned, then smiled sleepily. "Am I on the

floor?" Her eyes closed and she drifted off to sleep again.

Cursing softly, Eli scooped her up and set her on the bed. She was sick, that much was obvious. But how long had she been suffering? And what had caused her illness? Eli pressed his hand to her forehead, but it was cool to the touch. "No fever," he murmured.

Purple shadows tinged the skin beneath her eyes and her usually lush lips were dry and cracked. He grabbed a fresh bottle of water from his pack and returned to the bed, remembering his paramedic training from search-and-rescue.

He slipped his hand beneath her shoulders and sat her up. Reaching for her wrist, he gently pinched the skin on the back of her hand for a few seconds, then observed the response. "Lucy? Sweetheart? You need to drink something. Right now. You're dehydrated."

Eli opened the bottle and held it to her lips, then gave her a gentle shake. "Come on, honey, drink something for me."

She opened her eyes and looked at him. "Is it really you?" she asked again.

"It is. And I want you to drink this for me."

She groaned softly and shook her head. "I can't. It will just make me throw up."

"If you don't drink this, I'm going to call the helicopter and they're going to come and get you and take you to the hospital."

That seemed to get through the haze of her illness and she took a small sip. Over the next hour, he gently cajoled her into finishing the whole bottle, sip by tiny sip. She seemed to improve remarkably and when he left her to grab another bottle, she watched him from the bed.

He sat down beside her and she lifted the quilt and groaned. "I'm naked," she said. "Did you take my clothes off?"

"No, you did that on your own."

"When?" she asked.

"I don't know. How long have you been sick?"

"I'm not sure. How long have you been here?"

"A couple of hours."

She blinked in surprise. "That's all. It seems like days."

"Maybe you've been hallucinating. You must have had a fever." He cursed softly. "Why didn't you call for help?"

"I didn't need help," she said. She sighed. "It was just a stomach flu. Or maybe something I ate."

"When?"

"Tuesday night?"

"It's Saturday morning. You've been sick for three days. Considering your condition, you ought to be in the hospital right now."

"But you were here with me," she said. "You took care of me."

"Lucy, I just got here a few hours ago. I swear, you've been alone all this time."

The revelation seemed to confuse her and Eli had to wonder just how sick she'd been. So sick—and all alone. He sat down on the edge of the bed and took her hand in his. "Lucy, I really think you should see a doctor. Just to make sure you're all right."

"I feel so much better already," she said. "Now

that you're here." She paused. "Did you bring any-thing to eat?"

Eli chuckled. She was hungry; this was a good sign. Relief washed over him. He'd keep an eye on her and if she continued to show improvement, then he'd hold off calling in the cavalry. "I did."

He grabbed some food and a thermos from his bag, and when he returned to the bed, she was sitting up, the quilt tucked beneath her arms, her back resting against the pillows. "Day-old chocolate croissants," he said, drawing one from the bag. "And coffee. I didn't have a chance to get you a latte, sorry."

As he watched her nibble on the croissant, Eli real-ized how close she'd come to disaster. If she'd gotten ill just a few days earlier when no one was expect-ing to hear from her, he might have arrived to a much more tragic scene. This idea that she had to check in only once a week wasn't an adequate precaution.

He cursed himself again for letting down his guard. He'd been busy with his search-and-rescue duties in the past week—just when Lucy could have used a rescue. His instincts had been right all along. She shouldn't be staying here all alone, especially with no way to contact him directly for help.

"Maybe that croissant is too rich for your stom-ach," Eli said.

Lucy took a larger bite of the pastry and smiled. "Chocolate is the best medicine."

"Do you remember what you ate before you got sick?" he said.

"I think I know what I did wrong. I opened a can of mushrooms and they smelled a bit off, but I put them in the spaghetti sauce anyway." She wrinkled her nose. "Ugh, I should have known better."

"What else can I get you?"

"Do you have a hot shower in your backpack?" she asked. "I might almost feel normal if I could have a hot shower."

"Would a bath do?" Eli asked.

"I think it would," she said with a smile.

"All right, then," Eli said. He grabbed the last bottle of water from his pack and handed it to her. "Save your coffee and work on downing that."

Eli slipped out of the cabin and circled around to the rear, where his grandmother's old cast-iron cauldron was leaning up against the log wall. He remembered her using it for everything from laundry, to boiling off maple syrup, to heating bath water.

Lucy was about to experience a real backcountry bath. It was far from the height of luxury, but it would make her happy. It was all he could offer her. For now, it was enough.

It was the most unusual bath she'd ever taken. Behind the cabin, Eli had overturned an old cast-iron cauldron and built a fire beneath it, then filled it with water from the pump. When it was just the right temperature, he'd come back inside and found a clean sheet in the linen cupboard, then held it out to her.

"Close your eyes," she said, watching him warily from the bed.

"I've seen you naked before."

"Yes. But I don't think I have the strength to handle your reaction," she countered.

"You don't think I can control myself?" he asked. "Try me."

"I know you can't control yourself," she teased.

"I'll close my eyes if you close yours," Eli said.

She sighed. "All right, we'll both close our eyes."

"Deal," he said.

Lucy waited for him to do as she asked, then she crawled out from under the quilt. She watched him closely and the moment he began to open his eyes, she quickly shut hers. What difference did it really make? Besides, there was a certain satisfaction in knowing that he found her beautiful—even with the bags under her eyes and her hair stringy and tangled.

She stepped into his embrace and he wrapped the sheet around her body, tucking her against his chest. Lucy opened her eyes and grabbed the ends of the sheet, knotting the corners beneath her arm, but she didn't step away from him. Her gaze caught his and he stared down at her, his eyes focused on her mouth.

Holding her breath, Lucy waited, wondering if he was going to kiss her. "What now?" she murmured.

He blinked, as if startled out of his thoughts. "Where do you keep the soap? Shampoo? A washrag?"

"On the shelf above the sink," she said.

She wandered over to the front door and peered through the screen. The storm that had poured down buckets of rain earlier had quickly blown over and the sun was now shining across the meadow.

Though she did feel better, the illness had sapped her of her strength, and there were so many things to do—harvest logs for the new cabin, work on her garden, chop wood to add to the huge pile of split logs she'd need for winter heat. After three days off, she was probably months behind.

But now that Eli had arrived, her worry seemed to have dissipated. She'd spent the last month thinking about this day, wondering what it might be like between them. Would they fall back into the passionate relationship that had marked their last visit, or would they have to start all over again from the beginning?

Glancing down at her body, Lucy smiled. They'd managed to jump from awkward greetings to a nearly-naked body in no time. "Where are we going?"

He pulled up a weathered wooden chair and set it at the top of the porch steps. "You sit there," he said, setting the soap and shampoo next to the chair. "And I'll be right back."

When he returned, Eli was carrying two buckets. He set one down at her feet and then held the other over her head. "Ready?" he asked.

Lucy tipped her head back and closed her eyes. "Mmm."

The warm water sluiced through her hair and spattered on the plank floor of the porch. The sensation was exhilarating and soothing all at once, and in an instant, she felt as if the last traces of her illness faded into the haze of her memory. She held out her hand. "Shampoo."

"I'll do it," he said.

Lucy opened her eyes. "You're going to wash my hair?"

"Yeah, I can give it a try. How hard can it be? It's not that much longer than mine."

She closed her eyes again and lost herself in the

feel of his fingers gently massaging her scalp. If he was trying to seduce her then he was doing a damn fine job of it. Right now, she didn't require any sweet words or soft kisses. A man tending to her most basic needs was a much more powerful aphrodisiac.

"That feels so good," she murmured.

"Why didn't you call for help when you got sick?" he asked. "You could have died."

She shrugged. "I guess I didn't want them to make me leave."

"It's that important for you to do this?"

"Yes," she murmured.

"So important that you would put your life in danger?"

"I guess I didn't think my illness was that serious. I've been sick before and recovered. If you hadn't arrived this morning, I probably would have gotten up and made myself something to eat and continued on. I really am much better today."

"I should call your producers and tell them how sick you were. Maybe they'd rewrite those damn guidelines."

She looked up at him. "Please don't do that. I have to finish this. The right way."

"And how is that?"

"By myself. On my own."

"What's driving you to do this? Just give me a clue."

She didn't respond, and Eli shook his head, then turned to pick up the other bucket. "Close your eyes."

He rinsed her hair with the other bucket of warm water, then picked up the empty buckets and disappeared behind the cabin.

She had an answer to his question but it was so close to the core of who she was that it wasn't so simple to explain. She'd already lied to him about her teenage years, and though she trusted him, Lucy knew that he would look at her differently if she told him the real story. When pressed, she'd always said she was the daughter of a postman and a school-teacher. But Eli wouldn't believe that lie anymore.

Lucy sighed softly. Maybe it was time to give him the truth.

When he returned with two more buckets of warm water, she sat up and watched him as he kneeled in front of her, took her foot in his lap and began to lather up the washcloth with soap. He didn't realize that her foot was resting on his crotch, but Lucy was keenly aware that there was only a layer of denim between them and a very intimate touch.

"I've always needed to prove something to myself, to prove that whatever I want to do, I can do—alone."

"All right," Eli said. "That's part of the explanation. There's more to it than that, right?"

"Yes, it's what I expect once I accomplish something on my own."

"And what is that?"

"I expect to be happy with myself. Satisfied." She drew a ragged breath. "Maybe even…content."

"And you're not?"

"No."

He gently began to wash her foot, massaging the arch with the soapy washcloth. Gradually, he worked his way up her calf and over her knee. When he started on the other foot, Lucy sighed. "I lied," she said.

"About what?" he asked.

"At this moment, I'm completely content."

Eli chuckled softly. "It doesn't take much to please you." He grabbed her hand and pulled her to her feet, then started to massage her back and shoulders.

Lucy clutched the sheet above her breasts as she bent her head forward. The thin cotton was damp and clung to her skin, making it nearly transparent, but she was beyond caring. His touch had lulled her into a state of perfect pleasure.

Her fingers toyed with the knot of fabric that held the sheet to her body. What would he do if she simply let the sheet fall to the ground? Would he stop what he was doing or would he continue on, as if nothing had happened?

Lucy loosened the knot and the sheet suddenly dipped low on her back, the edge coming to rest just below her spine. His fingers stilled for a moment and then, he pressed a kiss to her bare shoulder. "Don't even try it," he murmured. "The last thing on my mind right now is seducing you."

"What is on your mind?" she asked.

"Finishing your bath. Making you something to eat. And getting you on the road to recovery."

"So you can seduce me?" she asked.

"Funny. I think the fever has messed with your brain. You've been too sick to have sex now."

Reconsidering, Lucy tightened the knot on the sheet. Maybe it was best to wait until she'd regained more of her energy. Every muscle in her body ached, she was still a bit light-headed and it felt like she had a sliver in her hip from the plank floor. But she still had an undeniable need to be close to him.

For so long, she'd refused to relinquish control. But here, in the middle of nowhere, all the rules she lived by no longer applied. With Eli, she could be weak and nervous and silly. She could indulge her every whim and no one would see her weakness. So why not?

She drew a deep breath, turned around and opened the knot on the sheet, letting it drop to pool around her feet. What he chose to do with her naked body was up to him now. Lucy smiled. And in truth, she was curious what he would do. Would his altruistic motives overwhelm his physical desires? Would nice or naughty win out?

He smoothed his hands over her shoulders and then down her arms. "I'm going to go get some more water." He handed her the washcloth and soap. "You can take care of the rest."

He was being strong for her sake, Lucy understood that. But sooner or later she would weaken his resolve and she would finally be able to make all of her fantasies come true.

"CAN I HAVE another cup of tea?"

Eli smiled to himself as he walked over to the bed and retrieved Lucy's mug.

After her bath the previous day, he'd helped her dress then changed the linens on her bed. She'd spent the afternoon curled up in the sun, reading one of his grandmother's Agatha Christie novels. After a light dinner of soup and bread, he'd tucked her into bed. She'd fallen asleep almost immediately and slept for nearly twelve hours.

"You look much better today," he said as he walked to the kitchen. "You have your color back."

"Are you saying I looked like a zombie before?"

"You're always beautiful."

Eli filled her mug with hot water and dropped a tea bag into it, then rummaged through his pack on the table until he found the satellite phone. When he returned to the bed, he handed her the mug and set the phone on her lap.

"What's that for?" she asked.

"I want you to have it," he said, sitting down on the edge of her bed.

"For what? I have the radio."

He nodded. "Yes, but the guidelines restrict how often you can use it. This phone comes free of guidelines. You can call me. I've programmed my cell phone number into the memory. You just hit Star-One."

"And then I can talk to you? Anytime I want?"

Eli nodded. "Anytime. Day or night. For any reason at all. If you call, I'll answer."

"Maybe I should give it a try," she said. Lucy set her mug down on the bedside table and picked up the phone. She pretended to push the buttons, then put the phone to her ear. "Ring, ring," she said.

Groaning, Eli reached into his pocket and pulled out his cellphone. "I don't have coverage up here."

"I know. Ring, ring."

"Hello," Eli said.

"Hello," she said in a playfully sexy voice. "It's me."

"Hello, you."

"What are you wearing?"

Eli chuckled softly. "A flannel shirt and jeans. What are you wearing?"

"Nothing," Lucy said. "Why don't you take off all your clothes and come over here. We can have a little fun."

With a soft curse, Eli grabbed the phone from her. "I'm serious about this," he said.

"So am I," Lucy said. "Take your clothes off."

He smoothed a strand of hair from her forehead and tucked it behind her ear. Though he knew she needed more rest and seduction was out of the question, that didn't stop him from needing to touch her at every opportunity.

He was afraid to leave her again, certain that the moment he did, something horrible would happen.

In all the time his grandmother had lived in this cabin, he'd never really worried about her safety. Even when his mother had taken off on one of her crazy adventures, he'd known that she was able to care for herself.

Lucy had proved that she was up to the task of living in the wilderness. So why was his brain always conjuring disastrous scenarios for her?

But he knew why. There was a vulnerability to Lucy, one she tried so hard to cover up. And that drew him. He wanted to heal whatever had hurt her so much in the past that she no longer trusted in anyone but herself. And he wanted to protect her from ever being hurt again.

"I'm going to stay another night," he said. "I just want to make sure you've completely recovered."

To his surprise, Lucy nodded. "I think that would be best."

"You do?"

She nodded. "I like having you here. And I've decided we can bend the guidelines a bit. Now will you take off your clothes?"

Eli gave her a gentle nudge and she slid across the bed, giving him room to lie down beside her. "I really should call air rescue and take you to the hospital to get checked out."

She reached up and smoothed her hand over his cheek. "I *am* feeling better. I promise, I'll tell you if I'm not."

He pulled her body closer and pressed his lips against her forehead. "I trust you. But I'm finding it harder and harder to leave you here alone."

"I'm perfectly capable of—"

He stopped her protest with a long, deep kiss. When he drew back, he nuzzled his nose against hers. "You don't need to remind me. This isn't about you. It's about me."

"How is this about you?"

"I enjoy being with you. One day a month doesn't seem to be enough anymore. I spend my days in town counting down the time until I get to see you again. And it's ridiculous. You're here and I'm there, but there's some silly reason why I can't just drop by for dinner every few days."

"It's a three-hour hike."

"Maybe I'll buy myself a helicopter."

She closed her eyes and pulled him closer. "This is all very strange."

"What is?" he whispered. He hooked his finger beneath her chin and turned her head so that she raised her gaze back up to his.

"I'm used to being on my own. I've never really had a—a relationship."

Eli frowned, staring at her in disbelief. "You've never been in love?"

"That, too. But I've never even had a boyfriend. There have been men, but it was just very…temporary. I don't—I haven't wanted to get involved—that way. Romantically."

Eli saw how hard it was for her to admit this truth and he didn't question her honesty. But he had to wonder how a woman as beautiful and smart as Lucy had never been in a relationship.

"My story is pretty much the same," he said.

Her eyes went wide and she smiled. "Really?"

Eli nodded. "And it seems to be genetic. The people in my family have an aversion to marriage and commitment."

Her fingers splayed across his chest and a long silence descended around them. Eli waited, sensing there was something she needed to say. He covered her hand with his, holding it to his heart. "Nothing you say to me is going to change how I feel about you," he whispered.

"I think it might," she said.

What could she be hiding? Did she have some scandalous past? A criminal background? Maybe she'd been married once. Maybe she still was. His mind started to spin with all the possibilities until the sound of her voice interrupted him.

"Remember how I told you that my father was a postman and my mother was a teacher?"

"I remember."

Suddenly, she pulled out of his arms and sat up beside him, breaking the physical connection between them. He reached out to take her hand, weaving his fingers through hers, but it was the only contact she'd allow. "That's not true. It's a big fat lie I tell when people ask about my family. I've said it so many times that it almost seems like the truth."

"What is the truth?"

"I've never said it out loud to anyone. And I'll understand if it changes everything for you."

"Is that why you're telling me? Because you want it to change everything?" He pushed up on his elbow and tried to catch her gaze, but Lucy refused to look at him. "For the good or for the bad?"

"Your childhood might have been strange, but mine was tragic. My mother died of a drug overdose when I was five. And my father went to prison for armed robbery when I was seven. My grandparents didn't want me, so I ended up in foster care. I ran away when I was fourteen. I lived on the streets for two years before I found a job with a production company and was able to afford rent and food."

"Jesus, Lucy, I—"

"I'm not telling you this so that you'll pity me. There was nothing I could do to change it. I'm telling you so that you'll understand why this, what's happening between us, is all so…impossible for me. I don't know how to be someone's girlfriend or lover or wife. I can't. And I'm just warning you ahead of time that you can't fall in love with me. It would never work."

Eli gave her hand a squeeze, then drew it to his lips and pressed a kiss to her fingertips. "I suppose I could give you the same warning. I don't exactly understand the whole happily-ever-after paradigm, either."

"I've been alone for such a long time, and it works for me."

He chuckled softly. "Me, too."

"So then you understand why I can't—"

Eli pressed a finger to her lips. "I do." He slipped his hand around her nape and pulled her into a deep, mind-numbing kiss. And he did understand; it was far too early in whatever this was between them to make plans for the future. For now, it was enough to lie next to her. But he already found it hard to be separated from her between check-ins. What would happen at the end of her year? He wanted to believe that they could have something once she came down from the mountain. "On the other hand," he began, "I'd like to think that I could change. Especially if I met the right person. And if I could change, then maybe you could, too. Not that I'm asking you to. It's just something you might want to consider."

"I don't know," Lucy murmured.

"Know what? Whether you can change, or whether you could consider it?"

"Both." She paused, then smiled. "But I do like kissing you. And I like touching you." Her hand smoothed down his chest, opening his shirt along the way. When she reached his jeans, she unbuttoned the fly and let her fingertips tease at the waistband of his boxers.

Eli growled softly as she worked his jeans and boxers down over his hips, a sleepy smile curling the corners of her mouth. He was already hard and when she wrapped her fingers around his shaft, his breath caught in his throat.

Never in his life had he felt as if he belonged, as

if he fit. But when he was with Lucy, everything fell into place so naturally. They seemed to know each other at a deeper level, as if their souls had met long before their minds and bodies had. He had no idea what her favorite color was or how she preferred her eggs. He didn't know if she could play tennis or if she got seasick. But he knew that they'd both been alone for a very long time—and now they weren't.

She drew back and pushed up on her knees. In the early-morning sunshine streaming through the window, her curves were lit with a soft filter.

Eli watched as she pressed a kiss to the center of his chest, brushing aside the faded shirt he wore. When she got to his belly, she ran her tongue along the length of his shaft, sending a wave of pleasure through his body.

"I guess you *are* feeling better," he murmured, pulling her hair away from her face.

"I bet I can make you feel better, too," she said.

He grabbed her waist and rolled her beneath him, pinning her arms on either side of them. "Why don't you save your strength and let me take care of you?"

He straddled her waist, trapping her beneath him, then bent closer and brushed his lips across hers. Lucy groaned, arching against him. When she reached for him, he caught her hand and held it above her head. "Stay very still," he whispered.

Eli slid his hand beneath the T-shirt she wore, exposing her belly first and then her breast. Eli grabbed the hem and slipped it over her head. Her skin was smooth and soft and he cupped her breast in his palm, teasing at the nipple with his thumb.

Lucy watched him, a smile playing on the edges

of her mouth. When he bent down and drew her other nipple into his mouth, she ran her fingers through his hair, gently smoothing her palm over his temple.

It amazed him how her touch held such power over him. A simple caress was enough to warm his blood and make him hard. Eli wanted to believe the touch was her way of silently communicating her affection, replacing the words she wasn't quite ready to say.

He moved lower, trailing warm kisses over her belly. Eli gently parted her legs and found the damp spot that drove her desire. His tongue slipped between her folds and flicked at her clit. Lucy sucked in a sharp breath and her fingers twisted in his hair.

He wanted to give her pleasure, to make her ache for him in the same way that he ached for her. Eli had always been a considerate lover, but with Lucy he wanted more than just a physical response. He wanted the connection that would only come when she was at her most vulnerable, when she'd look at him and he'd see the need in her eyes. It was a gift, as if she were entrusting him with her heart and soul.

Eli had always preferred a no-strings relationship when it came to women. But from the start, Lucy had wrapped him up in a tangle of desire and denial, until he had no choice but to surrender. Whatever she needed, he would give.

Eli brought her to the edge again and again but each time he pulled her back. She groaned in frustration and finally took matters into her own hands. With a wicked smile, she sat up and pushed him back with her foot until he sat opposite her, his arms braced behind him. She straddled his lap, slowly lowering herself until he was buried inside her warmth. She ran her hands along his shoulders and over his chest, the two of them facing each other.

As she began to move, Eli fixed his gaze on her face, watching the play of pleasure dance across her beautiful features. She knew instinctively how to please him, how to quicken her pace and then slow down, drawing her strokes out until they were exquisitely slow and filled with sensation.

Eli felt his orgasm begin to build. He reached between them and began to caress her. With a languid smile, she pressed her forehead against his and closed her eyes, twisting her hips as she came down on him. The change of movement sent a delicious surge of desire through his body.

Before long, they were both breathless, grasping for that one moment that they could share. He wrapped his hand around her nape and pulled her into a deep kiss and it was enough for him. Eli tumbled over the edge, surrendering to his pleasure.

As the last of his spasms faded, he opened his eyes to see her watching him, her eyes half-closed. Eli pulled out and laid her down on the bed, then brought her to completion with his tongue.

She shuddered with each wave of her orgasm. And when her body was finally still, Eli stretched out beside her and pulled her into his arms. "Are you all right? That wasn't too much?"

Lucy giggled. "Yes, you were far too good. Don't fish for compliments."

"I'm not."

"Let me give you a little secret. That thing you do

with your tongue. That kind of drives me wild." She pressed her finger to her lips. "Don't tell anyone."

He drew her closer and pressed a kiss to her forehead. "Since you gave me a secret, I think I should give you one."

"What is it?" Lucy asked.

"I'm not talking about the tongue thing," he said. "I mean what you said earlier about your past." He paused. "I like that we can be completely honest with each other. So, in that spirit, I want you to know that I've actually seen you more than once a month. I hike up here every week, just to check up on you."

She pushed up on her elbow. "You do?"

"I don't want to creep you out. It's not like I was stalking you. I just wanted to make sure you were safe."

"Why haven't I seen you?"

"I just come to the bottom of the meadow. And I wait until I you come outside and then I'm reassured that you're all right. Don't be angry. It's just that I take my responsibilities very seriously. And I feel responsible for you. Only, this past week I was busy with another job, and I didn't come. And look what happened. Once a month is definitely not enough."

She stared at him for a long moment and Eli couldn't read her expression. But then she reached up and cupped his cheek in her hand. "That's the sweetest thing anyone has ever done for me."

"You're not angry?"

Lucy shook her head. "No. Not at all. But from now on, you don't have to hide. You can come up to the cabin and at least say hello."

He leaned in close until their lips nearly touched. "Hello," he murmured.

"Hello," Lucy replied.

5

September

SUMMER IN THE ROCKIES was achingly short. The snow
had barely melted from the north face and the weather
had warmed just enough to grow the vegetables in her
garden before the cold set in again. Without warning,
the mornings turned chilly and spots of color marked
the maple trees along the edge of Trudie's meadow.

Lucy couldn't help but feel a bit melancholy. The
hardest part of her journey was ahead—the isolation
that snow and cold would bring. Next month would
mark the halfway point in her year and she couldn't
believe how much she'd changed in that time.

Since her illness, Eli had been coming to the cabin
more and more often. Though Lucy knew she would
have to send him away eventually, she was enjoying
his company. They'd grown so close as both friends
and lovers. Living here on the mountain, they'd managed to avoid the typical pitfalls that most couples
faced. There were no jobs, no family obligations, no

diversions to make them question the strength of their bond. They were simply…together.

They'd made no promises to each other. The future was just some vague point on the calendar. And though Lucy was happy not to complicate matters, she sensed Eli might not share her feelings.

He'd appointed himself as her protector, and had made it his mission to teach her what she needed to know to survive on the mountain. Yet, he knew well enough that he had to step back and let her take the lead with the "Trudie" project.

So while she refused his help in building her cabin, his advice had made the process go much more smoothly. He taught her how to sharpen the tools, how to create a roller system to move the logs faster and how to wield the log stripper so that it took off larger swathes of bark each time.

By the end of August, she'd collected enough logs to build four seven-foot-high walls and had started to notch the corners and fit the logs together. She was proud of the results of her efforts, and had documented every step of her progress with the camera.

Though it wasn't going to be the prettiest cabin and it was made with small trees that could barely be called logs, the important point was that it would be a shelter.

"I'm worried about the roof," she said, stepping away from her work to stare at the growing structure.

"You're not going to be able to put the roof on yourself," Eli warned. "My grandmother didn't. She had lots of help. And she had a horse to pull the logs down to the site. She had friends to help her put things together. She had a pulley system to put the rafters and the ridgepole in place."

"I know. But my cabin is much smaller than Trudie's. It's supposed to be crude. Look at the chimney. It isn't straight, but it's functional." She shrugged. "If it looked too good, they'd think I had help."

"Well, if you want to do a peaked roof," he said, "you're just going to have to tell your producers that you can't do it on your own. You could do a sod roof. Or, if you just had a slightly slanted roofline, you wouldn't need a ridgepole. Though, come spring, you'd have mud coming through the roof as the snow melts or when it rains."

"We can't do shingles, like Trudie's roof?"

"We'd have to cut some cedar trees and then split shingles. It would take a lot of trees and a lot of work. But you could work on that over the winter."

"I was hoping to live in it during the winter," Lucy said.

"Do you realize how cold it gets around here, Luce? And how windy? You'd be miserable."

"I never expected it to be anything less than difficult," Lucy said. He sighed and she sent him a warning glare. "Don't look at me like that. If I want to do it, I'm going to do it. With or without your approval."

"That's true, but here's the reality. With the materials you have and the time left, you're not going to get a perfect roof. It's going to leak when it rains or when the snow melts. Cold air is going to sneak into every little crack and crevice. And your fireplace isn't large enough to heat the entire cabin."

She sat down next to him, picking up the little bird he'd carved from a piece of scrap wood. Like her cabin, the carving was crude, but she still recognized it as a bird. "What would you do?" she murmured.

"I would get a canvas and put that over the roof. I'd turn your cabin into a workshop so that I could make shingles all winter long. And as soon as I had enough, I'd put on a proper roof."

He handed her his water bottle and Lucy took a long drink. "It doesn't look that bad, does it?" she asked.

"No," Eli said. "It has a sort of rustic charm that most people would find very appealing."

She nodded. "Yes, it does." A low rumble in the distance caught Lucy's attention and she frowned. "Is that thunder?"

Eli listened for a moment, then shook his head. "Nope. It's a helicopter. Maybe there's a search-and-rescue party out looking for someone."

The sound grew closer and closer and they both stood and turned toward the meadow. A few moments later, the helicopter appeared on the horizon, moving directly toward the cabin. Lucy's stomach lurched. "You'd better go," she said.

"Why?"

"It seems the producers are about to pay me a visit, and you're not supposed to be here."

"I'll stay," Eli said. "After all, they are the ones who are paying me."

Lucy hurried toward the cabin. "Fine, but I'm going to clean up your stuff from inside the cabin. You stay right there."

"I'll just walk out to the meadow to meet them," Eli suggested.

"No! You shouldn't even be here. It's not the first of the month."

"I'll just tell them I was…doing a few repairs around the cabin. I'm technically the landlord. I'm allowed to check up on my property."

"All right, but don't say anything else."

He gave her a teasing salute and headed toward the meadow, Riley trailing along after him. Lucy, meanwhile, raced around the interior of the cabin, hiding any evidence of Eli's presence. She hadn't realized until now that the two of them were virtually living together, his belongings comingling with hers.

By the time she'd finished and changed into clean clothes, Eli was escorting three people up the rise to the cabin. She hurried down the porch steps and met them halfway. Lucy recognized the two women, Rachel McFarlane and Anna Conners, as her producers, but they'd brought along a man.

"Hello," she said. "This is a surprise."

"We wanted to catch you in your natural habitat," Anna said, a bright smile on her face.

"You've met Eli Montgomery," Lucy said. "He's Trudie's grandson. He stopped by to—"

"To fix the seal on the water pump," he said.

"Yes," she said.

"And now that I'm done, I'm going to head out. Miss Parker, I'll see you next month."

"Do you really have to leave?" Rachel asked.

"I have a long hike back down," he said.

"We could take you down on the helicopter," Rachel said.

"No, I'd rather hike."

"Your pack is on the porch," Lucy said.

Their gazes met for a moment, before Lucy turned to the stranger in the group. "I'm Lucy Parker."

"This is Bennett Sinclair," Rachel said. "He's a programming exec from the Lifeworks network. He's very interested in buying our show, but first he's got some new ideas that we'd like to discuss with you."

"New ideas?" Lucy forced a smile. "From a man?"

"The gals here told me about how you only wanted women on this project," Sinclair said. "Well, unfortunately that will have to change. We're concerned that the existing format doesn't provide enough drama for a cable reality show, and I'm here to push things along. But don't worry, your idea is in good hands. I've worked in television for twenty-five years. Trust me. I know what I'm doing."

Rachel gave her a gentle pat on the back. "Why don't you show us around and we'll get to Bennett's ideas later?"

Lucy stole a quick glance at Eli as he passed by her. He gave her a wink and a wave and she wanted to stop him, to ask him to stay. He could explain the problems with the cabin roof. Or he could explain the fireplace design. Lucy groaned inwardly. She hadn't realized how much she'd come to depend on him until now.

She waved at her cabin. "Well, as you can see, the walls of the cabin are up. Then I figure we'll have the first few weeks in October to do the chinking before the freezing cold weather sets in."

"You need a roof," Sinclair said.

"Well, I have a couple of options there. I'd like shingles, but I may have to settle for sod."

"Yes, that's good. Sod is dirty and full of worms and bugs. More drama."

Over the next few hours, she played tour guide, taking the trio from her new cabin to her garden to the smaller projects she'd been working on inside the cabin. Rachel and Anna seemed to be impressed by the pickled radishes and beans she'd canned, and Sinclair questioned her about possible botulism from home canning and the human interest it might provide.

She talked about Trudie and recalled sections of her diaries, pointing out some of her things in the cabin. But Sinclair didn't seem every interested in the history of the cabin. Instead, he seemed more concerned with the bear population.

He asked a long series of questions about how much of a danger the bears were to her, about what bears ate and when bears were most active. Lucy had a hard time reading the motives for his questions. When he moved from bears to other wilderness threats, Lucy offered up the story about her illness. She left out the part where Eli had rescued her, but Lucy's version seemed to pique Sinclair's interest.

"We've brought along a picnic lunch," Anna said. "Why don't I set it up on the porch and then we can get down to business."

"Business?" Lucy asked.

"Yes," Rachel said. "We have some important matters to discuss about the show and we thought it best to come here personally and talk to you about them."

Though she couldn't read Sinclair, it was clear that Rachel was not happy with what they'd come to say. She sent Lucy a smile, then an apologetic shrug.

"I'll just get some plates and forks."

As she moved around the kitchen, she heard the backdoor squeak. Eli popped his head in. "Everything all right?" he asked.

"Go away!" she whispered. "They're out on the porch."

"Don't look so scared. Be tough. Show them what you're made out of."

Eli disappeared and she sighed softly. His words had made her feel a bit better. This was *her* project. She'd conceived it and brought it to them. She'd sold it to the producers and she wouldn't let some network guy stroll in with his plans to change things up. She'd just need to stand her ground and everything would be fine.

Lucy walked back outside and found Sinclair and her two producers deep in conversation. When they saw her, they split apart and Sinclair stepped forward. "I'm just going to make this short and sweet. The show needs more drama. More excitement. Or no network will buy it. What you've given us so far isn't a reality show. It's a sleep aid. You have to crank up the excitement. If you don't, you might as well pull the plug." He glanced back at Anna and Rachel, who both looked stricken. "But I have some great ideas for how to turn this ship around. All right? Let's start with the bears…"

He talked all through lunch about various traumas that Lucy could endure over the next six months. Somewhere around his enthusiastic description of Lucy's possible encounter with a rabid porcupine, she realized that there would be no standing up to

Bennett Sinclair. Her project, as she'd conceived of it, was finished.

Shoving his now empty plate at her, Sinclair put an end to further discussion. "Well, this meeting has been very productive. I'm glad we're all on the same page about the new vision for the show."

He walked off the porch and headed for the helicopter. As Anna and Rachel passed her, they each gave her hand a squeeze.

"Can he do this?" Lucy asked.

Anna nodded. "If we want the show to be seen, we need him."

As the trio walked to the helicopter, Lucy glanced down at Riley, who sat by her side. "Maybe you could fight a mountain lion," she muttered. "That would be dramatic."

"HE THINKS I'M BORING, ELI. He's watched the footage I've shot and he says I'm about as exciting as—a sleeping pill!"

Eli gently rubbed Lucy's back. "Why does he get a say? You and the producers decided what the show would be. Why aren't they sticking to the plan?"

"Anna and Rachel say that if we play it Sinclair's way, his network will buy the show. They see this as their big chance. I guess they're capitalists first and feminists second."

"But it's your idea."

"It seems they agree with Sinclair. If I don't change things, they're going to pull the plug. I mean, I can continue to live here and do my videos. But there would be no money for postproduction or marketing. I'd be left with just a bunch of home movies."

Eli's anger surged. Why hadn't he stuck around to talk with the TV people? He could have defended Lucy's idea and explained what his grandmother might have wanted. He could have offered assurances that Lucy was working hard.

"You can fix this," he said. "There are lots of interesting things you can show the audience without compromising the integrity of your show. I'll help you."

"There's another thing. They want to send a cameraman. They think my taping doesn't look slick enough. And that my tape will be more dynamic if I don't have to worry about the camera. So, there's probably going to be another man on the mountain before too long."

"Not necessarily," Eli said. "I've worked as a cameraman before. On a trekking expedition in Mongolia. Maybe I could talk them into hiring me."

Her expression brightened. "Really?"

"Yeah. I'd be the perfect choice. I know the area. I'm used to living in rugged conditions. And I happen to be sleeping with the star of the show."

"We could do this together," she said.

He pulled her close and gave her a hug. "See. That's not so bad."

"They also asked if I had an ex-boyfriend."

"An ex-boyfriend?"

"Sinclair suggested he could show up and try to convince me to come home to add a romantic interest to the show. The man is all about drama. I swear, he'd dognap Riley if he thought it would create suspense."

"Well, an ex would add an interesting element. What did you tell them?"

"That none of my exes would be interested in the

job. He said they could always hire an actor." She cursed softly. "This show was supposed to be real, not some reality cliché fabricated for maximum conflict. Next thing you know, they'll be bringing in trained bears and mountain lions to wander around the property. Sinclair seemed obsessed with bears. I think he's really hoping that I'll get mauled and we'll be able to catch it on film."

"Come on," he said. "Let's get out of here for the day."

"Where are we going?"

"Where would you like to go?"

"A luxury hotel with a spa," she muttered.

"Done. I can call a friend of mine with a helicopter and he'll have us off this mountain within the hour."

"You'd really do that for me?"

"Sure. If it would put a smile back on your face, I would."

She threw her arms around his neck and kissed him. "We could spend the afternoon in bed. That always makes me smile."

"I have a better idea. We can stay in the wilderness, but get away from the cabin for a while. I'm going to take you camping. And trout fishing."

"Will it be dramatic?" she asked.

"Oh, yes, trout are very good fighters. And we will have to kill them before we eat them, so I suppose blood and fish guts could make it even more dramatic."

Over the next half hour, they gathered food and clothes for their trip, along with a few basic cooking utensils that Lucy put in a smaller day pack. Eli noticed her mood lighten almost immediately and before long, she was laughing and teasing, excited to learn how to fish.

He helped her lift her pack onto her shoulders, then handed her the rifle and attached the bear spray to the waistband of her jeans. Once he'd hefted his own pack onto his back, he stepped out onto the porch. He whistled to Riley, and the dog jumped up from his place on the porch and fell into step with both of them.

"Do you need a compass?" she asked.

"I know where we're going. It's not that far. About an hour hike."

They walked across the meadow, hands linked. The weather was perfect, the sky blue and the sun bright. Eli couldn't think of a better way to spend the day than tramping through the wilderness with Lucy.

Life seemed to be so easy on the mountain. But Eli had to wonder whether it would be the same once they both went back to the real world. For now, this was her job, but if she was involved in television production, then she'd need to live in Los Angeles or some other large metropolitan area. He'd never lived in a city in his life. He'd been through almost every major airport in the world, but he'd never bothered to step outside and see the city around that airport.

"When this project ends, what are you going to do next?" Eli asked.

"I don't know," Lucy said. "I mean, when I started this, I thought it would be a stepping stone to something much bigger. But living here on the mountain has changed me."

"How?"

"I've learned to live in the moment. I've learned how to quiet my mind and notice the beautiful things all around me. I guess most people do that when they're kids, but I never could. My childhood was a constant battle. I always had to be on guard. Here, I can just be myself."

He slipped his arm around her shoulders and pulled her close. "I wish you could have met my grandmother. She would have loved you."

"I've been thinking about her a lot lately. Sometimes, I can feel her presence. Not her ghost, but… her spirit. The other day, I was pulling carrots from the garden and I thought I heard a laugh. It was probably just the wind in the trees."

"It could have been Riley," Eli said.

She laughed. "Now that you mention it, he does make a funny sound when he yawns. But I wanted to believe it was her and that she was watching over me, like some fairy godmother. I never had that, someone who cared about me. You're lucky. You actually knew her."

"She wasn't always easy to get along with," Eli explained. "She was incredibly stubborn and opinionated. And she treated men as if the only thing they were really good for was sex and lifting heavy objects. But she squeezed every ounce of enjoyment out of her life. When she found something that made her happy, she just immersed herself in it until something new caught her fancy." He drew a deep breath. "And she never compromised when it came to things that were really important to her."

In truth, the person he described sounded a lot like Lucy. But Lucy was vulnerable in a way that his grandmother never had been. Lucy's confident exterior hid what was left of the terrified child she'd once been.

Eli wanted nothing more than to fix that child, to make her life whole again and to reassure her that everything would be all right in the future. He'd come to care about Lucy and yet, he knew their future might end the moment she walked off the mountainside.

But did he even want a future with Lucy? What did that mean? Would they live together? Would they get married and have a family? Though he didn't know everything about Lucy, he knew that those sorts of ideas were not a part of her plans.

Would it be enough for him if they were just lovers? Though a no-strings relationship had always seemed ideal to him, with Lucy it would be easier said than done. He certainly didn't enjoy the thought of her with another man.

He glanced over at her. Maybe all this confusion was a result of a unique confluence of events. She seemed perfect for him because everything around them was perfect. But take the two of them off the mountain and nothing would be the same.

"I'm not going to compromise," Lucy said. "I'm going to do this the way I wanted to do it. And I've decided that I'm going to weave a biography of Trudie into the narrative. This is going to be a tribute to her."

"That's a wonderful idea," Eli said.

"You'll help me, right? I mean, you knew her. I'll need to do a lot of research. Maybe you could introduce me to Buck?"

"Yeah. He has some pretty colorful stories about Trudie."

"Great. That's decided then. We can try to get better footage, do more interesting things for the camera. But that's it. I'm not going to ruin a good idea. That would be selling out."

Eli gave her shoulders a squeeze. After everything she'd been through in her life, she still had such an incredible inner strength. She knew exactly who she was. And the more he learned about her, the more he wanted to learn.

"Are you sure we're not lost?"

"I know exactly where I'm going," he said.

For now, he was moving forward. He was going to enjoy the time he had with Lucy and hope it turned into something more than just a friendship with incredibly pleasurable benefits. He planned to do everything he could to prove to her that they belonged together—off and on the mountain.

"This is how you fillet a trout in eight or nine easy steps," Eli said. "First, you put your trout on a flat surface then take your knife and…"

Lucy stared down at the fish lying on a flat rock, the silvery skin shining in the late afternoon sun. They'd been lucky with the fishing, but cleaning the fish was something she really wasn't interested in doing. No doubt it would involve lots of smelly and slimy stuff.

Still, she wasn't about to let Eli see her reluctance. So she'd have to touch fish guts. She'd faced far worse things in her life.

"Are you listening?"

"What?" She glanced over at Eli. "Yes. No. I was just thinking about what a nice little life this fish was living just an hour ago. Swimming around in that beautiful river with all his fish friends. Maybe we should have just let him go."

"Well, we don't have that option anymore. This fish and his three friends are dead and we're not going to waste them."

"A multiple murder," she muttered. "Now, that's drama. Did you get this on tape?"

"Funny," Eli said. "We have four very lovely rainbow trout here and nothing for dinner. You tell me, how would you cook them?"

"I would put them on a stick and roast them over the fire."

"Why don't you cook it your way and I'll do it my way and we'll see whose fish tastes better?"

"All right," she said.

"But first you have to clean the fish," he said.

"I can't cook it with the guts in it?"

"No." Eli handed her the knife, then held up his hand. "Wait, let me get the camera."

Over the next half hour, Eli filmed the fish cleaning and fire preparation from several different angles. When it was his turn, he quickly cleaned his trout, then showed her the complicated process of removing the bones. After that was finished, he washed it in salt and a bit of water from their canteen, then grabbed the burdock leaves that he'd picked earlier.

"Roasting fish over a fire is one way to cook your catch. But you can also wrap it in burdock leaves," he said. "Then you push some of the hot coals aside and drop the little package of leaves and fish into the fire."

Lucy put her fish on a forked stick and found a place to prop it up near the fire. She'd cooked fish before, but never directly from its original home. Eli had already put his fish in the fire and was seated on a log he'd dragged close to the heat.

"So we have a little contest going here," she said, plopping down beside him.

"It's not a contest," Eli said. "My fish is going to be the best."

"You can't guarantee that," she said. "I might just have some mad fish cooking skills you don't know about."

This brought a laugh from Eli. "Sweetheart, I've been cooking trout since I was six or seven years old."

She gasped, then twisted around to face him. "Sweetheart? Did you just call me sweetheart?" She got to her feet and stared at him, her fists hitched up on her waist.

Eli winced. "All right, that might have come out of my mouth, but it's not what you think."

"I think you were talking down to me," she said.

"Well, I'm sure that's what my feminist grandmother might say. But *I* would say that I was merely using a fairly common term of affection. Sweetheart? Sweetie? Darling? Babe?"

"Babe? Really. You consider me a babe?"

"Well, yes. You kind of are a babe. If I were hanging out with a bunch of guys in a bar and you walked in, we would definitely refer to you as a babe."

Lucy opened her mouth to cast back some disparaging remark about the quality of the friends he had, then stopped herself. She'd been on the defensive for such a long time that she might not be able to recognize a simple expression of affection. Or a compliment. "What does a woman have to do to qualify as a babe in your book?" she asked.

"In my book? Well, she has to be beautiful. But not necessarily in the conventional sense. I'm attracted to women who look beautiful even without all the paint and pretty clothes. Like you when you wake up. Your eyes are still a little sleepy and your hair is all falling in front of your eyes and your lips are pink against your pale skin. I've never seen a woman more beautiful than you are in the morning."

Emotion surged inside of Lucy and she swallowed hard. No man had ever called her beautiful, or spoken to her in such a sweet and kind way. Was this really how Eli felt or was it simply another weapon in his seduction arsenal?

Lucy sat back down and folded her hands in her lap. "All right, you're forgiven."

"Does that mean you don't mind if I call you babe? Because I really prefer babe to sweetheart."

"You can call me whatever you'd like," she said.

"All right, babe," he said.

She glanced over at him to find him grinning at her. He might find this entire conversation amusing, but Lucy found it deeply confusing. These affectionate names were something that had meaning to most people, they were sentimental expressions that people shared when they were close to each other—when they loved each other.

Though she was certain that Eli wasn't in love with her, she could tell that his affection for her had deepened since they'd first met. With every day that passed, the bond between them was becoming stronger, deeper, more resilient. And now, she wondered if she might have let it all go too far.

Lucy quickly stood up. "I'm going to check on my fish," she said.

As she brushed past him, he grabbed her hand and pulled her down into his lap. Cupping her cheek in his palm, he drew her closer until their lips met in a sweet and gentle kiss.

Lucy stared into his eyes, the flickering fire reflected in the pale blue depths. She trusted him completely and that had never happened with anyone else in her past. She realized it was dangerous, but it felt so good to share her life with someone who would never betray her.

Eli opened her jacket and then her shirt, pulling aside fabric until he'd exposed one of her breasts to the cool air. He flicked at the nipple with his tongue, drawing it to a peak before moving to the other breast.

"What about our dinner?" Lucy asked in a breathless voice.

"We've got another fifteen or twenty minutes," he murmured. "I have an idea of what we can do in that time." He grabbed her hand and pulled her toward the tent.

"We're not going to have sex now," she said.

"Of course not. Twenty minutes isn't nearly enough time for that."

"Then dinner can wait." There were more urgent needs that would be met first.

She crawled inside the tent and he followed, tugging off her boots as she lay back on the down sleeping bags. Lucy watched as he unbuttoned and unzipped her jeans, then pulled them off and tossed them aside. Grabbing her legs, he yanked her closer, pulling her knees up on either side of him.

Then, with a wicked smile, he pulled her panties aside and slowly began to touch her, his fingers gently massaging her sex. Lucy groaned, bracing herself on her elbows as she watched him seduce her with a single-minded purpose.

By now, Eli had figured out exactly how she liked to be touched and he used that knowledge to his advantage. But Lucy had let him control their sex life for too long. She wanted to take her share, to learn every response and to pleasure him with as much skill as he pleasured her.

She gently pushed him back into the sleeping bag and worked his jeans down to his hips. Lucy smiled up at him, then ran her tongue along the length of his shaft. He grew hard before her eyes, and she urged him on with her tongue.

He tried to touch her, but she deftly pulled away. Then she bent close and blew on him. A shudder raced through his body, like a jolt of electricity.

A few moments later, her tongue flicked at the tip of his penis, sending another jolt through his system. The cold had made his senses much more acute and the contrast of her warm mouth and the frigid air heightened his pleasure.

She used her tongue and her fingers to gradually bring him to his peak and even when he tried to stop her, Lucy wouldn't be deterred. Eli braced himself, his hands clutching her shoulders when the first spasm hit.

The sticky warmth of his orgasm pooled on his belly and when he was finally spent, he glanced down at Lucy, her hand slick. "Look what you've done," he said.

"Don't worry. I've got some burdock leaves that will clean that right up."

He laughed, then pulled her up until she was stretched out over the length of his body. "That was a very nice appetizer."

"And it took twenty minutes. It's the perfect timer for fish." He kissed her and Lucy melted into his embrace, two becoming one.

But that was the problem, wasn't it? It was what she'd feared from the very beginning. That having Eli at the cabin would change the project—would change her. And Lucy feared that soon she'd no longer recognize herself.

6

October

THE MOOD IN the cabin had been tense all morning. Eli and Lucy had awakened to a fresh coating of snow on the meadow and the first snowfall had brought Lucy's spirits crashing down.

Her cabin wasn't close to being done. The sod roof was nearly complete, but they hadn't finished cutting the sod and once the ground froze solid, they wouldn't be able to continue.

In truth, Eli was glad that the cabin project could finally be put aside. Though Lucy had worked so hard on it, the rush to finish it had put too much of a strain on her—and on their relationship. She'd worked in the cold and in the rain, until she was nearly exhausted, refusing to accept any help from him beyond the occasional bit of advice.

The production company had sent a new camera so that Eli could document her progress, but he didn't like watching her gradually fall apart through the view screen. Strangely enough, the producers seemed much more enthusiastic about the latest batch of video. They were getting the drama they wanted, but it was at the expense of Lucy's well-being.

Right now she was curled up in his grandmother's old rocking chair, peering out the window at the snow, her feet tucked beneath her. With a deep sigh, she pushed out of the chair and walked over to the door, slipping her feet into her boots. The wind had picked up and the temperature had dropped, but she was still determined to go out and work.

"Stop," Eli murmured.

She turned to face him. "How many times are we going to have this same argument? There's too much work to do. I can't stop. I need to finish."

"Why? Lucy, you can't live out there. The place has only got half a roof. The snow is coming in. Some of the chinking has to be redone, although at least the holes will be easy to find because the wind will blow through the walls. And you don't have either a door or windows."

"Well, maybe if we wouldn't have spent so much time fooling around I would have finished it by now. Do you have any idea how many hours we wasted in that bed?"

Eli shook his head. God, she was just spoiling for a fight, but he wasn't going to oblige. "I don't consider that time wasted." He pushed the chair back and stood. "If you want to get the cabin done, then let's do it. I'll help you. We'll work until we finish it."

"No," she said. "I have to do it myself."

"Then you're not going to finish. Winter is coming and you can't finish the cabin when you're knee-deep in snow. I suggest you accept the fact that the cabin will have to wait until spring and move on."

She grabbed her jacket and slipped into it, then shoved her hands into her gloves. "Come on, Riley."

The dog looked up from his spot next to the fire, then yawned and put his head back down on his paws.

"Even he doesn't want to go outside," Eli said.

Lucy leveled her gaze at him and he could tell that he'd pushed her too far. "Why don't you just go home. Pack up your things and leave. If you're not going to be supportive, then I don't want you here."

She stepped outside and slammed the door behind her. Riley sent Eli a doleful look and then closed his eyes and continued his nap. Eli walked to the stove and poured himself a cup of coffee from the old blue enamel pot. He sipped at the hot brew as he paced the cabin, trying to decide his next move.

He'd been contracted by the production company as a cameraman, and since he'd started, the producers had charged him with the responsibility of finding interesting subjects to tape. But the tone of the emails had changed recently. The network was losing interest in the show. They had already mentioned to Eli that they might only need him through Christmas and then they might be calling a wrap.

Eli had tried to renew their enthusiasm for the project. He'd insisted that the winter would provide much more excitement and conflict. Plus he was going to teach Lucy how to hunt and trap, and he'd brought her a small shotgun, perfect for squirrels and rabbits and other small game.

Sinclair had been excited about the shotgun, but Lucy had refused to use it, preferring to exist on the dried beans and canned vegetables that she'd originally stocked in the pantry.

Eli knew she had a soft heart and was sympathetic to the furry creatures of the forest. But as a result, most of the drama happening at Trudie Montgomery's mountain cabin was happening between Lucy and her new cameraman. And much of that was his fault.

He hadn't mentioned to Lucy that he suspected the production company was about to pull the plug. He'd been trying to spare her feelings, but maybe if he told her, she'd give up a few of her stubborn ideals and try to work within her limits. She could still make an incredible show, but it didn't have to revolve around her finishing that damn cabin.

Frustrated, Eli walked to the door and picked up his own jacket from the hook on the wall. As he slipped through the door, he pulled his gloves on, then grabbed a warm cap from his pocket and tugged it down over his ears.

He found Lucy in front of her cabin, her attention completely focused on sawing a length of wood for her front door. He noticed that she'd already attached one plank to the crossbars. But even if she finished the door, the cabin was still wide open to the elements. Right now, a door seemed like a ridiculous frivolity for a cabin that only had half a roof.

"Have you come to cheer me on?" she asked, an edge of sarcasm to her voice.

"Can we just talk for a few minutes? There are a few things I need to tell you."

"You can talk while I work," she suggested.

Eli grabbed her elbow and gently turned her to

face him. "Just a few minutes and then I'm going to head out."

"You're going to hike back in this snow? No. You can go in the morning if it's clear, but I'm not going to spend my time worrying about you getting caught in a blizzard."

"We could always hike out together," he suggested. "You, me and Riley. You could use a few days in civilization. Besides, you wanted to interview Annalise. It would be the perfect opportunity."

She looked up from her work. "Is that all?"

"No. I spoke with the production team earlier this week. They're starting to discuss when we might want to wrap this project up."

"The project will be done April first of next year."

"Well, they're considering shutting you down at the end of December."

Lucy gasped. "They told you that?"

"It was pretty clearly implied that if I had other job offers after the first of the year, I should take them."

The energy seemed to drain from her body and she sat down on a small bench. "Could we change their minds?"

"I don't know, Lucy. Maybe, but I don't think you should count on it."

"It's my fault. I thought I could do this. It was a good show until they changed direction. I wanted it to be simple and intimate, like a personal conversation with Trudie. They want it to be…silly. I should never have trusted them. Anna has always wanted to move up in the ranks and Rachel is in it for the money."

He reached out and grabbed her gloved hand, then laced his fingers through hers. "If they decide to cancel it, then you will just carry on. Do what you came here to do. Does it really matter anymore if other people see it? Maybe this was always meant to be between just you and Trudie."

She turned to face him. "I'm going to be fine," she said. "You can go back inside."

"Are you going to come in?"

"Not just yet. I'm going to finish this door. And then I might just paint it blue because I've always wanted a house with a blue front door." She held on to his hand, her fingers toying with his. "Maybe I should try to find some new investors. There's got to be someone out there who'd be interested in this."

"I'm sure there is," Eli said. "Why is this cabin so important to you? It seems to be about more than just experiencing life as my grandmother did."

"What else would it be?" she asked.

"I'm no shrink, but if I were to guess, I'd say that you're trying to build yourself a home—maybe because you've never had a home of your own?"

She forced a smile. "You're right. You're no shrink." Lucy stood up and went back to work on the front door. "Go inside before you freeze. The wind is picking up."

Eli knew he wouldn't accomplish anything further here. He'd make dinner for them both and perhaps they could continue their conversation over a few glasses of wine. Her single-minded pursuit of this idea was all good when everyone had been on the same page. But now it was time to consider a new direction.

As he walked back to the warmth of his grandmother's cabin, he realized there was another way to make this all work—but in order to finish the project the way Lucy wanted to finish it, she'd have to compromise everything else she believed in. Eli didn't want to force her to make that kind of choice, but they were about to run out of options. So now, he just had to figure how to convince her of the beauty of the plan without kicking him out of her life forever.

"Who wants to be a millionaire?" he murmured as he walked inside the cabin. "Maybe I do."

LUCY WORKED UNTIL the last trace of light had disappeared from the sky, until her fingers were so cold they barely moved. She looked around at her cabin and tried to fight back a flood of tears.

She wasn't even sure why she was upset. Hell, she never let anything get to her and couldn't remember the last time she'd cried. Crying was a manifestation of weakness and she would never allow herself that kind of self-indulgence.

Her life used to be so simple. Everything existed in black and white. Now everything seemed to be fraught with emotion. Even this silly log building with its half-done roof and its nonexistent windows. But it wasn't just the cabin, or the project, or her life. It was him.

Lucy sat down on the rough-hewn bench and wrapped her arms around herself. Since the visit from her producers, she'd been trying to understand why she felt so out of control. And then she'd realized it was Eli. Everything was about Eli. They were so inextricably twisted together that she didn't know who she was without him anymore.

So she'd been trying to separate herself, to go back

to who she was when she'd first arrived on the mountain. But it had been impossible. That Lucy Parker no longer existed. She'd been changed.

Now, she had two choices. To walk away and try to find the life she used to have, or to learn to live as a person who cared. A person who cried and fought and maybe even loved. Could she strike down the walls she'd built and open her heart to something new?

Lucy stood up and shoved her gloved hands into her jacket pockets, then trudged through the snow back to the cabin. As she climbed the porch steps, she turned around to stare across the meadow, the grass now covered with a pristine blanket of snow, a riot of stars in the sky above her.

A soft light poured out of the windows of the cabin and she could see Eli moving around inside. He'd wanted to leave earlier, but she was glad he'd stayed. Solitary nights in Trudie's cabin just weren't as satisfying as they used to be. She liked having him in bed beside her.

Lucy opened the door and stepped into the dimly lit interior. A fire was blazing on the hearth and the oil lamps around the cabin were flickering. The scent of dinner filled the air and she drew a deep breath and sighed.

Without a word, Eli crossed to her and helped her remove her jacket and boots. Then he gathered her in his arms and kissed her, his lips gently teasing until she finally surrendered the last bit of her anger. It still surprised her how a kiss or a caress could completely alter her mood.

Eli hugged her, nuzzling her neck. "You're freezing."

"It's cold out there."

"It's going to get a lot colder," he said. He pulled her along to the fire and settled her in the rocker, then tucked a quilt around her body. "I made chili. Are you hungry?"

Lucy nodded. As Eli got her something to eat, she pulled off her wool socks and let her frozen toes thaw, resting her feet on the edge of the stone hearth.

She'd come to love the quiet at the end of the day. In the summer, they'd strolled through the meadow and in the fall, they'd sat on the porch, dressed in heavy sweaters and jeans. And now that winter was upon them, they'd retreated to the cozy warmth of the cabin with its crackling fire and creaking wood floors.

Eli handed her a mug and a spoon, then sat down on the edge of the hearth, facing her. "Did you finish the door?"

"I just have to fasten the strap hinges on it, but it's together. Not that it's going to do a lot of good."

She dug into the chili and sighed as the warmth worked its way through her body. Though she was a passable cook, Eli was much more comfortable with camp meals, making something good out of dried and canned ingredients. He was, by all accounts, a handy man to have around.

"Maybe we should hang the door tomorrow morning. I could get some good footage of it."

She smiled. "Now you've changed your mind? You don't think the cabin is a waste of time?"

"I was wrong," Eli said. "You need to make your own decisions about this. My opinion doesn't matter."

"Don't say that," Lucy countered. "It does. I just

reserve the right to ignore it." She set the soup mug on the hearth, then got up and wandered over to the bed. Exhaustion overwhelmed her body and she pulled the covers back and crawled inside, still dressed in her jeans and sweater.

Eli followed her, stretching out beside her and wrapping his arm around her waist. "I don't want you to worry about the producers pulling the plug on this project. I've figured out a way around that."

"Are you going to beat them up until they agree to do it my way?" she asked.

"No. If they don't want to do this your way, then we should just buy the project back from them. Return their investment and take control."

"That's a lovely idea, but I don't have the money to do that and neither do you—"

"But I do," he said.

She stared at him, puzzled, and he realized he hadn't fully explained. "My mother recently told me that as Max Quinn's son, I'm entitled to some money."

"The inheritance you mentioned a few months ago?"

"Yes, from my great-aunt, the Irish novelist Aileen Quinn. All I have to do is pass a DNA test, prove I'm a Quinn and then I get a million dollars. There is the small possibility I may not be Max Quinn's son, but my mother assures me it's pretty tiny."

"That's amazing. But it's your money."

He brushed a kiss across her lips. "Yes. And I'd be giving some of it to you. To make your program about my grandmother. I have a vested interest in this, too."

The temptation was nearly overwhelming. It would solve every one of her problems. She could continue on here for the rest of her year and not have to worry about anything except doing what she originally set out to do. He was giving her a free pass and she ought to grab it and run.

And yet, every instinct deep inside of her screamed at her to refuse. She'd lived her entire life fighting for what she wanted and needed. No one had ever given her a handout or a hand up and Lucy was proud of that fact. To take his money would be to admit she'd been defeated.

She ran her fingers through his hair, then pulled him into a long, deep kiss. Her tongue traced the crease between his lips and with a groan, Eli pulled her beneath him, the kiss intensifying.

He was the kindest, sweetest man she'd ever known. And yet, he held the power to consume her. He'd been chipping away at her resolve from the moment they'd met, making her more and more dependent upon him. And now, he wanted to make her financially dependent on him as well.

There were times, like this, that she wanted to drop the weight of living her life and let someone else deal with her problems. It would be wonderful to let her guard down. "I'm still cold," she murmured.

He kissed her again. "Maybe I can do something to fix that," Eli said. "They say, in the case of hypothermia, you should take off all your clothes and find a nice warm body to use for heat."

"Who says that?" she asked.

"I don't know. But it sounds like a good idea. And I'd be willing to be the body if you'd be willing to take your clothes off."

"I might be too tired to take off my clothes," she said.

Eli sat up and took her hand, pulling her to her knees. Slowly, he undressed her, discarding each piece of clothing before exploring the exposed skin with his lips. Lucy smoothed her hands through his thick hair, watching as he lazily seduced her.

Was surrender her only option with Eli? How much longer could she fight him? Sooner or later, she'd have to admit how much he meant to her. Without her even being aware of it, he'd carved out a spot in her heart. And now, she wondered if she could live without him.

A deep ache stole her breath for a moment and she wrapped her arms around him as his lips found her breast. There were moments when she was with him when all the pain and tragedy that she'd experienced in her life just melted away. Moments when she felt as if she could begin her life all over again.

As he slipped inside her and began to move, Lucy arched against him, desperate to feel the weight and the heat of his body. The familiar anticipation began to build and she started on the slow climb to her release. Before long, she'd drifted into a world of pure sensation and instinctive response.

But how long could this go on? How long would she crave him so deeply that it defied all reason?

ELI SAT AT a leather chair at the end of a huge conference table, staring at a piece of abstract art that looked suspiciously like a donkey riding a bicycle. Aileen Quinn's representative had called a week ago to set up the appointment, and Eli had assumed that meant his DNA test had checked out. The guy wouldn't make a trip all the way from Ireland to tell him that he wasn't a Quinn, would he?

The conference room overlooked the main office and Eli watched as the staff, all dressed in serious suits, buzzed around like bees in a hive. He'd never in his life wanted to work in an office. To keep regular nine-to-five hours seemed like a prison sentence to him.

Yet, it was easy to shun the corporate world and a regular paycheck when it was just him. When a guy took on a wife and had a family, everything changed. He suddenly had to provide a comfortable and secure future for those he loved.

Not that he'd seen any of that when he was a kid. He and Annalise had always lived hand-to-mouth. When there was extra money, it had gone to his mother's climbing expeditions. Buck and Trudie had provided incidental cash, and once Eli was old enough to work, he'd supported himself. But that was back when minimum wage seemed like a million bucks to a teenager.

Now he had a million bucks, more money than he could make in twenty years. But was it enough? It was plenty if he lived off the grid at the cabin, plenty if he carefully invested the majority of it. But in the real world, even a million wouldn't last a lifetime.

A slender man dressed in an impeccable suit hurried into the room. He held out his hand. "Hello. My name is Ian Stephens. I'm here representing Aileen Quinn."

"Eli Montgomery," he said. Eli stood and shook the other man's hand, then sat down. Another lawyer followed Ian in and sat at the opposite end of the table, quietly taking notes, even though nothing had been said beyond the greeting.

"I'm glad you decided to contact us," Stephens said. "Miss Quinn is quite anxious to welcome you into the Quinn family."

"I'm not sure I'm a Quinn," he said. "I mean, even if there is Quinn blood running through my veins, I don't have any kind of connection to the family. They're just names to me."

"I certainly can understand that, Mr. Montgomery. But the results of the DNA test do indeed prove that Maxwell Quinn is your father. That means Conal Quinn is your grandfather. And Malcolm, Rogan, Ryan and Dana Quinn are your half brothers and sister. As a Quinn heir, Aileen Quinn is determined to take care of you."

"Funny. I've never heard that name before in my life. Conal? You can understand that I'm having a hard time taking this all in."

"Yes, of course. Maybe this will make it easier?" He held out an envelope.

Hesitantly, Eli took it, then opened the flap and withdrew the check. There it was. Nearly half a million dollars. And his name was typed on the check. "Wow."

"As we discussed earlier, the other half of your inheritance will be given to you upon your visit to Ireland. Miss Quinn has made a point of visiting with every one of her brothers' descendants and we hope you'll be no exception."

"I'm afraid it's going to be a while until I can get there," Eli said. "I'm in the middle of a project right now and won't be able to get away until May or June."

"Miss Quinn is in her late nineties. The sooner you can visit, the better." He held out his business card.

"Call me and we'll make all the travel arrangements to and from Ireland."

"Ireland," Eli said. "I'm Irish."

"Indeed you are. And you have quite a number of relatives all around the world, many right here in the States." Ian stood up and closed his briefcase. "Well, it was a pleasure meeting you. I look forward to welcoming you to Ireland."

"Thank you," Eli said, staring down at the check.

Ian pushed another envelope across the table, this one a larger manila packet. "I thought you might enjoy this, as well. It's some information about the Quinn side of your family. About your half siblings and some of your cousins."

The man smiled, then briskly walked out of the room, leaving Eli with the ever-silent lawyer. Eli grinned and held up the check. "So, how much of this do I owe you?"

"Nothing, sir. Mr. Stephens took care of my fee."

"What do I do now?" Eli asked.

"I'd suggest you visit the bank," the lawyer said as he stood. "Can I get you anything, Mr. Montgomery?"

"No. I'm just going to sit here for a while and let this all sink in. Is that all right?"

The lawyer nodded. "Perfectly fine."

Eli stared down at the check, reading the amount over and over again, as if it might just change in front of his eyes. He'd never wanted anything from his father, not that it had ever been offered. At one time, it had helped to be angry that he'd been ignored. But at this point in his life, it was reassuring to know where he came from. That he had siblings, that he had roots.

And there were things he wanted to do, and some

of those things required money. This money came without strings, beyond a short trip to Ireland to meet a distant relative. This money could buy a whole new life for himself. A life that included Lucy.

He jumped up from the table and grabbed his jacket from the back of the chair, then headed for the door. If he wanted to get back to the cabin before the sun fell, he'd need to leave soon. But as he stepped outside, he realized a quick hike to the cabin was no longer in the cards. Another snow squall had moved in.

Glancing down at the check, he smiled. He didn't have to hike anymore. Hell, within the hour, he'd have half a million dollars in the bank. He could get home to Lucy in style. He could also bring along a few luxuries, things that wouldn't fit in a backpack.

"Eli!"

He turned at the sound of his name and saw his mother approaching, dressed in a trendy winter jacket trimmed in fur. When she caught up to him, she threw her arms around his neck and gave him a fierce hug. "I'm glad I ran into you. I've left at least ten messages on your cell phone."

"I've been up at the cabin. They hired me to do some camera work and I—"

"Yes, I heard. I also heard about your meeting this morning with the lawyer. Are you rich now?"

"Yeah, I guess you could say that."

"Good. I know you've never been interested in that side of the family, not that I've encouraged you. But at least you've gotten something positive from it."

"If you need anything, Mom, I'd be happy to—"

"Don't be ridiculous. It's your money." She paused.

"But you might want to give a little to your grandfather. Buck has been struggling a bit lately. He's supposed to have knee surgery but he's been putting it off because he can't afford it."

"I'll go see him today," Eli said.

Annalise smiled and pressed her palm to Eli's cheek. "I'm so happy for you. This money will make your life easier. It will give you opportunities. You can travel the world. Where are you going to go first?"

"I think I'll be staying here for a while," Eli said.

"Here? But you hate it here."

"I meant I want to stay at the cabin. I've got this job that's supposed to last through the winter. And I like spending time up there and—"

Annalise gasped. Then a slow grin spread across her face. "Are you sleeping with Lucy Parker?" She watched him with a shrewd gaze then laughed. "Oh, my God, you are. So that's where you've been spending all your days. Well, this is an interesting development."

"And it's also none of your business. I'd appreciate it if you'd keep the news to yourself. I don't want the producers hearing about it. They may want to include it in the show."

Annalise slipped her arm around his. "It'll be our secret—as long as you take me out for breakfast and tell me all about it."

"I'm not going to talk about it."

"Do you love her?"

Eli opened his mouth to answer then realized he didn't really have a reply for that question. In truth, the reply changed daily, hell, sometimes hourly. Was he falling in love with Lucy? Maybe. Probably. More and more with every day that passed. Did he love her? That was a bridge he hadn't yet crossed.

"I have to stop at the bank and then I'm going to see Buck. We'll have breakfast another day. I'm going to be around for a few more months."

She pushed up on her toes and gave him a kiss. "Let's do dinner, then. I want you to meet Richard."

"I thought you and Richard were fighting."

"Oh, he made a lovely apology and took me to Las Vegas for a little getaway weekend. Then I took him to Death Valley and we went hiking."

"Nice," he said. "I'm glad you're having fun."

Eli got into his truck and pulled out into the street. After a stop at the bank and lots of good wishes from the employees there, he headed to the edge of town and a rustic A-frame where his grandfather, Buck Garrison, resided.

Like his grandmother's cabin, Buck's place was home to Eli. He'd spent most of the year sleeping in the loft bedroom while he attended high school. Buck had been the closest thing he had to a father and he could always count on him for good advice.

Eli rang the doorbell and a few seconds later a shout came from inside. "I'm comin'. Hold yer water." When the door swung open, a huge figure filled it.

Buck was a massive man, a wall of muscle and sinew. Even at age seventy, there wasn't an ounce of fat on his body. His once-black hair was now a shock of white, and his dark skin was still nearly smooth, owing to his Native-American ancestry. He was a for-midable figure with a charming nature that attracted women young enough to date Eli.

"Well, what we have here? You look something

like a grandson I once had. I heard you were back in town."

"Stop," Eli said. "I know I haven't been around lately, but I've had a good reason."

"You goin' to tell me what that reason is?" Buck asked.

"I will if you'll let me in," Eli said.

Buck stepped aside and Eli walked past him. The interior was a typical bachelor pad—dark wood, leather furniture and a large-screen television over the fieldstone fireplace.

"How's the knee?" Eli asked.

"I hope to hell you didn't come here to talk about my knee because I've got nothin' to say about that matter," Buck said, lowering himself into his favorite leather recliner.

"I've been spending a lot of time out at the cabin."

"I heard about the business going on out there. I'm not sure Trudie would approve," he muttered.

"I don't agree. I think she'd like Lucy Parker. They're very similar." Eli paused. "You'd like Lucy, too. Actually, she was hoping to interview you. I'm hoping you'll agree."

Buck waved his hand. "Yeah, yeah."

"Can I ask you a question, Buck? How come you and Trudie never got married?"

Buck didn't seem startled by the question. He just sighed and shook his head. "I've been trying to find an answer to that question since I met Trudie. I guess I missed my chance. I think there might have been a time she would have accepted my proposal, but somehow, I missed that time."

"Did you ever ask her to marry you?"

"No. Never seemed like the right moment. Trudie was always off on one mission or another. We'd fight and then we'd come back together again. She just seemed happy with the way things were."

"Were you happy?" Eli asked.

Buck thought about the question. "I reckon I wasn't. But I was willing to take what I could get. She was a powerful, beautiful force of nature. Like a summer thunderstorm." He sighed softly. "I remember the day we met as if it was yesterday. I was nineteen. She was twenty-four. She said she liked the way I looked so she took me home and had her way with me. Nine months later, your mother arrived." He paused for a long moment. "I did love that woman."

"How did you know you loved her?" Eli asked. "Did it just hit you one day or did it come on gradually?"

"Both. It came on kind of slow, but then it hit me like a truck. I realized she was the only one I'd ever want and that was that. Why all the questions?"

"Lucy asked me about you and Trudie. I want you to meet her."

Buck frowned. "What's goin' on with this girl? Are you sweet on her?"

"I guess I am," Eli said.

"Well, take my advice. If you want her, you better put a ring on it."

Eli chuckled and shook his head. There weren't many seventy-year-olds who could quote Beyoncé. "Well, that's about the best advice you've ever given me. Put a ring on it."

"It's what I shoulda done," Buck said.

Eli wasn't sure that Lucy was the marrying kind.

From everything that he knew about her, she was as unconventional as the two other women in his life. But Buck was right. There would come a time when he'd have to tell her how he felt—that he wanted her in his life. If he said it too soon, he'd scare her away. And if he said it too late, she'd already be gone. But, if he managed to make his proposal at exactly the right moment, he and Lucy might be together forever.

7

November

"IT'S FINALLY FINISHED."

Lucy stood outside the rough log cabin, staring up at the facade. Eli stood nearby, the video camera trained on her.

"I wasn't sure how I'd feel when it was done," she said. "I remember cutting down the first tree. It took me an entire day of chopping with an ax and then it was too heavy for me to drag over here, so I had to cut a smaller one." She glanced over at the camera. "I know it doesn't look like much, but it's—" She swallowed back a sudden flood of emotion.

Why was she getting all teary eyed? Lucy wondered. This was the moment she'd been waiting for, the culmination of a lot of hard work and determination.

"How *do* you feel?" Eli asked.

She pasted a smile on her face. "Great," she said. "Amazing."

"Then why are you crying?"

"I'm not crying," Lucy said.

"Your eyes are all watery."

His gaze was fixed on the view screen of the video camera and Lucy held up her hand. "Just stop. Don't tape this."

Lucy needed a moment to gather herself. But Eli continued to watch her through the camera. "Be honest," he said. "Just say what you feel."

She drew a deep breath. "Please, just turn it off."

Lucy spun away and started toward the big cabin, trudging through the snow. Her breath clouded in front of her face and a tear froze on her cheek. She didn't want to cry in front of him. She'd done that once before and it had only made her feel silly and weak.

She ought to be more grateful to Eli. After all, he'd been the one who'd arranged for the helicopter to drop off the building supplies for the roof and the windows. Once she'd had plywood and cedar shingles, she'd been able to finish the roof. And the three windows had been surprisingly easy to install. The resulting cabin wasn't pretty, but it was something she'd done with her own two hands. It was a home—the only home she could ever claim as her own.

"Come on, Luce!" Eli called. "Come back. I'll turn off the camera."

She brushed the tears from her cheek and walked back to him. Eli pulled her into his arms and hugged her tight. "What's going on?"

She shook her head. "I'm just a little sentimental," she said. "It's silly."

"Why do you always do that? Anytime you get emotional, you say that you're being silly. You're entitled to your emotions, Lucy. Why can't you just accept that? You don't always have to be so tough."

"Old habits die hard," she said.

"I can see that. Now, tell me how you feel about your cabin being finished. No cameras. Just us."

She drew a ragged breath. "I thought I'd be happy, but I'm really sad."

"Why?"

"This cabin feels like my home. The only home I've ever had. Except that it's not my home and I'm not going to live here." She looked up at him, smiling through her tears. "I told you it was silly."

"So, do you want to give me a tour?" he asked. "I haven't been inside since you put the doors and windows in."

Lucy nodded, then took his hand. When they got to the front door, she paused. "It still needs some work. I'm thinking of bringing in a decorator. And the wall-to-wall dirt floor is the wrong shade of brown, but I'm going to have that refinished."

"If I go home with you, will you promise to take advantage of me?" he asked.

"We'd have to do it standing up. I don't have any furniture."

"I could handle that," Eli said.

She pushed open the door but before she could step inside, Eli grabbed her waist and scooped her up into his arms. Then, with great ceremony, he carried her across the threshold. "What are you doing?"

"I'm carrying you across the threshold for good luck," he said.

Lucy laughed. "Newlyweds do that when they

move into their first home. It's luck for the marriage, not the house."

Eli dropped her on her feet. "Sorry. I didn't know that. But I do have this." Reaching into his jacket pocket, he withdrew a bottle of champagne. "This tradition is all right, yes?"

Lucy took the bottle from him then kissed his cold cheek. "Where did you get champagne?"

"I bought it last month. I thought we ought to have a bottle in case we had something to celebrate. Or christen. I guess we could do both with the cabin. What will it be? Drink it or smash it?"

"I think we should drink it," she said.

Eli slowly circled the perimeter of the small cabin. Though the structure wasn't heated yet, it did provide shelter from the wind and the cold.

"As you can see, the place has central air," Lucy said.

Eli chuckled. "It is nice and cool in here."

"And it comes with this lovely roof, which will protect you from rain and snow, unless it leaks. Then it won't."

"But then it would have running water and that's a positive, wouldn't you say?"

"True. We also have these wonderful windows, made of one hundred percent real, authentic glass. They provide this lovely all-natural and organic light."

Eli slipped his arms around her waist and rested his chin on her shoulder. They stared out at the snow-covered meadow. Lucy drew a deep breath. "I don't care what's wrong with it," she said softly. "I think it's perfect."

"Let's sleep here tonight," Eli said. "We can make a fire in the hearth and throw a canvas down on the dirt floor. The down sleeping bags will keep us warm enough."

"No, it's all right," she said. "It's enough that I've finished it. My cabin is done. Now, no matter what happens, I can walk off this mountain without any regrets."

"You don't have to walk away," Eli said. He grabbed her hand. "Even if they pull the plug on production, you don't have to leave. You can finish your year here. I'm not going to kick you out. You can still complete your goal."

The prospect of losing their production funding had been looming over her since he'd mentioned it last month, though in reality she'd started to be concerned after the producers had visited the cabin in September. She and Eli had tried to come up with more exciting content. They'd documented the last phases of building the cabin, they'd focused on cooking and baking, they'd added more material from Trudie's journals. They searched out more flora and fauna. In truth, she and Eli had stayed up late into the night coming up with ideas that might appeal to network viewers.

The only feedback she'd received was that she should leave her hair loose while on camera because it was sexier, and they'd suggested that a small amount of makeup would help highlight her eyes. It was a small compromise to make just to keep the project on track, but it didn't give Lucy much confidence that she'd still be at the cabin by the spring. Or that the show would ever make it out of postproduction.

There was the other option that Eli had suggested, but Lucy couldn't quite bring herself to consider it. With Eli's windfall inheritance, he'd offered to continue funding the project if the producers and the network decided they didn't want it. Though it was a generous offer, Lucy couldn't bring herself to accept. If she couldn't make this work, then she needed to accept the fact that she'd failed. There was no shame in failure.

Yet, there was a small part of her that knew if she did accept his help, it would tie them more closely together, and that option was becoming more agreeable.

She'd tried to imagine her life without him—returning to Los Angeles, finding a new job, moving on with her career. He was the first real friend she'd had. And the first lover who'd made it past the one-month mark. There weren't men like Eli Montgomery standing on every street corner.

"I'm going to try the fireplace," he murmured, pressing a kiss to her cheek.

She followed him outside to help him gather firewood and kindling from the stack against the west wall of the big cabin. They carried it inside, and Lucy sat down on the dirt floor to watch him stack the wood in his very precise way.

She'd learned so much about him over the past five months, but it all revolved around this specific spot, a place where he was entirely comfortable. A place where they didn't have to worry about money or jobs or all the other stresses of life. What would happen when they went out in the real world? They couldn't possibly be the same people, could they?

Eli sat back on his heels as the flames licked at the

kindling. Before long, the smaller logs had caught and heat radiated out into the room. To Lucy's delight, the flue drew the smoke up the chimney perfectly, taking it all up and out.

"I have an idea," he said. "I'll be right back."

Lucy stared into the fire. It was so hard to imagine herself anywhere but here. She'd learned to love the soft light from a blazing fire, the smell of coffee on a cold morning, the call of an eagle echoing overhead. This had become her life and it was difficult to picture herself walking away from it. Trudie had found peace on this mountain and now Lucy had as well.

But was she prepared to give up everything she'd worked for to stay here? For the remote possibility that they'd be able to make a life here work? Eli returned a few minutes later, his arms full. He spread a canvas on the floor, then tossed the sleeping bags on top, making a comfortable spot for them to sit. Next he handed her a bag of giant marshmallows. "What are these for?"

"Dinner," he said. He'd brought along a couple of long forks, then reached in his pocket and produced a couple of mugs for the champagne.

"Marshmallows and champagne?"

"Perfect combination. White and fluffy. Clear and bubbly. The happiest food and drink on the planet." He sat down in front of the fire, then patted the spot beside him. Lucy plopped down on the ground. "Why don't you work on dinner and I'll pour the drinks."

As he peeled the foil off the cork, Lucy began to stick the giant marshmallows onto the forks. "I always wondered what these forks were for," she said. "I figured they were for spearfishing." She pulled on the handle, then smiled. "I get it now, though. The handles are long so you don't have to be right next to the fire.

He turned to stare at her. "Haven't you ever roasted a marshmallow before."

"No." Lucy shrugged. "There are a lot of things I've never done. I had a strange childhood. I can't ride a bike. I don't know how to swim. I never went to the prom. When we went camping in the summer? That was the first time I'd ever slept in a tent."

"We're going to have to work on all of that. There are a lot of things I haven't done, either, though. I never built a cabin with my own two hands. I never met a woman more beautiful than you. And I've never wanted a year to last forever." With a smile, he handed her a mug of champagne.

It was the most unconventional celebration Lucy had ever had. Eli taught her the special skill of roasting a marshmallow, how to hold it far enough from the flame that it didn't burn but close enough that it didn't take too long to roast. How to slowly turn it so it browned evenly. How to find the very best spot in the fire for roasting.

They drank the entire bottle of champagne and fed each other marshmallows until late into the night. And when it came time to sleep, they zipped the sleeping bags together and crawled inside.

Facing each other, they held hands. "This has been one of the best days of my life," Lucy whispered. "I'm glad you were here to share it with me."

It had happened over and over again in the past few weeks, the urge to tell him how much he meant to her. The words *I love you* weren't that far off. She could nearly feel them on her tongue. And she almost believed the truth in them.

"TODAY I'M GOING to use the snowshoes I made last week to do some tracking in the woods." Lucy doubted she'd run into a rabid porcupine, but she hoped the tape of this trek into the woods would excite the network people. "I don't have to walk far to find wildlife around the cabin, but to be able to identify animal tracks is something new for me. I'm using this book I found in Trudie's library—*North American Animal Tracks* by William Donaldson. I'm strapped into my snowshoes and I'm ready to go."

Eli continued to follow her with the camera, but when she didn't move, he switched it off. "That was good," he said.

She looked down at her feet and took a tentative step. "How am I supposed to walk in these? It feels like I have two giant frying pans on my feet."

"You have to pick up your foot and place it down carefully. The snowshoes will distribute your body weight so you won't sink into the snow. But if you step on the edge of the other shoe, you'll fall down. Give it a try. One step at a time."

"Don't you dare tape this," she warned as she began to walk.

"Oh, don't worry. This won't be the only time you fall."

"How do you know I'm going to—" Lucy pitched forward and her legs tangled beneath her. There was no way to catch her balance with the huge snowshoes strapped to her feet and the only choice she had was to collapse facedown in the snow.

Riley leapt off the porch and bounded through the snow, jumping on top of Lucy and digging in the snow around her until she rolled over.

She looked up at Eli, her face covered with snow, and he couldn't help but laugh. Lucy cleared her face and held out her hand for help. But Eli shook his head. "No, you need to be able to get up on your own. You built a log cabin alone, you can certainly get yourself up and out of the snow."

"If you're taping me I'm going to throw that camera in the nearest snowbank," she warned again. She struggled to stand and when she finally got upright, she bent over to brush the snow from her legs. But Riley jumped up against her and she lost her balance once more, this time falling sideways.

"This would have made such a great YouTube video," he said. "It would have gone viral."

This time, she only made it halfway up before falling. Eli decided to give in and help her to her feet. At this rate, they'd never get out into the woods. But when he took her hand, she gave it a yank and he fell down into the snow beside her.

Lucy took a handful of snow and rubbed it in his face, then lay back and stared up into the sky, her breath clouding in front of her face. "Have you ever seen a sky so blue?" she asked. "It's the most beautiful thing."

"I'm looking at something more beautiful," he murmured.

Eli leaned over and kissed her snow-chilled lips. He couldn't imagine that there could be another woman in the world who would make him any happier. He'd never believed all the sappy stories about love and romance and how meeting the right person could change your life. But it had happened to him.

From the moment he'd first met Lucy, there'd been an undeniable connection, as if they'd known each other much longer than a few minutes. From that point on, all he'd wanted was for Lucy to recognize that connection.

There were times, like this, when it seemed as if they were madly in love. And yet, the mood could shift in a heartbeat, leaving Eli to question whether it was all in his imagination. He'd come to the point where he needed to know how Lucy felt about him.

"Stay here with me," he said.

"I can walk in these things," she said. "I swear. It'll just take a little more practice."

"No," Eli said. "I mean stay here, on the mountain, with me. When it comes time to leave. Stay."

She gave him an odd look. "I—I don't understand."

He smoothed his hand over her cheek. "We're good here together, Luce. And I'd like to see where this goes, no matter what happens with the project."

"But you don't live here," she said.

"I could. Over the past few months, I've realized what this place means to me. How good life can be when you can focus on the small things...the real things. And having you here makes it so much better."

She pushed up on her elbows, her gaze fixed on his, as if she was trying to read some unspoken truth in his eyes. Should he tell her that he loved her? Would that make a difference? Was it even true?

"How would it work?" she asked.

"I have the money," he said. "A million dollars can last a lifetime if we live off the grid. And think about it. The two of us together could really make a life here work. Every day could be an adventure."

"Is—is this a proposal?"

"Yeah. I mean—" Eli stopped, the real meaning of her words suddenly sinking in. She meant a marriage proposal. "Would you like it to be a proposal?"

"No!" she said, sitting up and shaking her head. "We barely know each other. And I've never even thought about getting married."

"Never?"

"No. Not beyond the fact that I'm sure I'd be horrible at it. I couldn't spend my life trying to make someone else happy while I grow more and more unhappy."

"Right," he said. "I completely understand." Eli found himself scrambling to salvage something from his offer. "Just think about it. If you don't have any plans after you're done here, I mean. I'm considering staying and—"

Lucy scrambled to her feet. "If you're going to stay, maybe you could keep Riley."

"You're giving me your dog?"

"No, no. He's not my dog. He's a production dog. They adopted him from a shelter so I'd have someone to talk to when I wasn't talking to myself. I can't have a dog in my regular life any more than I could have a husband. I don't have a home and I don't have anywhere to keep him. Please say you'll adopt him. I couldn't live with myself if they sent him back to the shelter."

"Sure," Eli said. "Yeah, I can keep him."

"Good." She forced a smile. "We should go." With that, she turned and started toward the meadow at a quick pace. To his surprise, she moved with a newfound ease, placing each step carefully in front of the other.

"That went well," he murmured.

Riley sat at his side, his body covered with snow, his liquid brown eyes gazing up at Eli.

"I wanted a woman and I ended up with dog. How did that happen?"

He crawled to his feet and brushed the snow off his pants and jacket. Perhaps he hadn't made himself clear to Lucy. Maybe he ought to tell her how he felt about her. "I love you," he murmured. "I love you."

It wasn't that hard to say. But how was he supposed to be sure he really meant it? Maybe no one was ever sure. Maybe everyone took a chance and if it worked out, then all the better. Lucy was the only woman he'd ever even considered inviting into his life, so that had to mean something, right?

He tucked the camera in his day pack and then adjusted the strap of his rifle on his shoulder. Life with Lucy Parker would never be boring, that much was certain.

"Come on, Riley."

He followed her tracks in the snow, his eyes fixed on her slender figure. Somewhere along the way, he'd missed the memo about how to carry on a romance with a beautiful and smart and sexy woman. He understood the seduction part but he had no idea how to get past that to the happily-ever-after ending.

This is what came from growing up with two women who didn't need men in their lives and one man overburdened by the torch he carried. Was that how Eli would end up? Like his grandfather—spending his life mourning the woman he could never have?

LUCY STARED AT her old video camera sitting in the middle of the room. Eli had mounted it on a tripod and left her with instructions to work on a cooking segment for Thanksgiving, which was just a few weeks away. She'd been flipping through Trudie's journals, looking for hints about how the other woman had celebrated the holidays. But instead, Lucy had gotten distracted, reading bits and pieces about Trudie's love affair with Buck Garrison.

The thoughts Trudie had expressed in her journal were so honest and so intimate that Lucy had to wonder if the older woman had ever expected anyone to read her journals. And yet, according to Eli, that was the type of woman she'd been. Unafraid of her feelings and passionate about the life she'd chosen to lead.

The more Lucy read about Trudie's life, the more she understood her. Trudie had been a complex human being, filled with contradictions and frailties that weren't always evident to the casual observer.

Lucy crawled out of the rocking chair and walked to the old dresser near the bed. There was just one journal left and she was afraid to open it. She suspected it chronicled the last days of Trudie's life, when she'd known that she was dying. Lucy wasn't sure she could handle saying goodbye to a woman that she'd come to admire more than anyone she'd ever met.

Trudie Montgomery had lived her life on her own terms, had been a woman who'd never cared what society expected of her. And yet, she'd had her secret insecurities and her unspoken doubts, just like Lucy. But if Lucy was searching for answers to her own questions, she hadn't found them in the journals.

"Maybe we're all just a little screwed up," she said, placing the journal back on the shelf. She picked up a framed photo, an old black-and-white snapshot that rested among the items on Trudie's dresser. She'd looked at it before and admired the joy that seemed to radiate from the image.

The woman in the photo was Trudie and she couldn't have been any older than Lucy was now at the time it was taken. She was sitting on the lap of a handsome man, dark-haired with a striking profile. They'd been caught in an embrace and their expressions said everything that words couldn't.

She studied the male and then realized that it had to be Buck. There was something about the smile that reminded her of Eli, in those moments when his mind was set on seduction.

She drew a deep breath and let it out slowly. Would she have a photo like this when she was old and alone? Would that photo be of Eli? Lucy pressed her fingertips to her lips and fought back a flood of tears. She didn't want to live her life and then realize that she had only one regret.

Lucy walked to the fireplace and held out her hands to the glowing embers. Eli had left yesterday, hiking back into town with their laptop computer. For some reason, the satellite linkup had stopped working. They hadn't been able to upload any video footage for at least a week.

And now she was alone again, the way she'd been in those first months on the mountain.

In truth, she was happy for the solitude. Living with Eli could be a bit exhausting. And they'd been working so hard on the project that she was grateful for a few days away from the video camera. "Thanksgiving can wait," she murmured.

She tossed another log on the fire, then walked to the woodstove to make herself a cup of tea. Suddenly Riley, who'd been sleeping near the fire, leaped up from his spot and ran to the door, barking loudly.

Startled, she dropped the teakettle back onto the burner and hurried to the door. Eli had said he'd be gone for at least three or four days, planning to stay in town while his grandfather had knee surgery. But he must have come back early. Lucy couldn't help but feel a bit of relief. Lucy threw open the door, ready to greet him with a kiss, and Riley ran out. But the dog didn't greet Eli. Instead, a slight figure dressed in cold weather gear stood at the bottom of the steps.

"Hello!" she said, brushing the hood off her head.

"Annalise! What are you doing here? Is everything all right? Is Eli okay?"

"Oh, he's perfectly fine," she said, kicking off her snowshoes. "May I come in?"

"Of course," she said. "It's your cabin."

"Actually, it's Eli's. His grandmother left it to him in her will. I never quite understood my mother's fascination with this place."

Lucy shut the door behind her. "Can I make you a cup of tea? I have some blackberry scones I made earlier."

"I *am* famished. It's a good hike in the snow and cold. Not very challenging, but a nice bit of exercise."

"Why did you come?"

"I thought you and I might have a nice chat while the boys are occupied," she said.

"You hiked four hours in the middle of winter for a chat?"

"Darling, I've climbed Everest twice. The hike here is practically a...well, a walk in the park. And it only takes me three hours."

Lucy pulled out one of the chairs from the table. Annalise slipped out of her pack and set it against the wall near the door, then took off her jacket and hung it up.

"How is Buck?"

"Oh, ornery as ever. But the surgery went well and he's recovering nicely."

Lucy couldn't help but wonder what Eli's mother had come to say. Annalise Montgomery didn't seem the type to hike three hours in the cold just to chat about her father and the weather.

Lucy placed a scone in front of the older woman and then brought out a plate of butter. "We usually don't have butter, but Eli brought some back after his last trip into town. He prefers real butter on his popcorn. It's one of our few indulgences."

"It sounds like you two get along quite well," Annalise said.

Lucy grabbed a clean mug from the shelf above the sink and dropped a tea bag into it, then added hot water from the teakettle. "We have honey but only powdered milk."

"Honey is fine," Annalise said.

Lucy prepared her own tea, then took a spot across the table from Eli's mother. In any other circumstance, she'd be peppering Trudie's daughter with questions. But Lucy sensed that the other woman had come here for a specific reason.

As if Annalise could read her mind, she straightened and set her mug down. "Why don't we get right down to business," she said.

"Business?"

"My son. It's quite clear to me that he's fallen in love with you. But Eli isn't the kind of man who expresses his feelings with any great regularity. He's my son and even I don't have a clue how his mind works. He's never really had a girlfriend, at least not one who's lasted more than a month. Only now, he seems to be quite taken with you."

"We're just friends," she insisted. "Ask him and he'll tell you."

"Of course he won't. I'm his mother. He never confides in me. But I know you are much more than friends. I love my son and I don't want to see him hurt. So, what are your intentions?"

"My intentions? I have no intentions regarding your son."

Annalise observed her shrewdly. "None? Why not? He's a wonderful catch. He's smart and kind and he knows how to treat a woman."

"I completely agree. I'm the one who isn't a good catch," Lucy admitted. "I'd be a horrible partner for anybody. I can't make him happy, I'd make him miserable."

Annalise took a slow sip of her tea as she seemed to consider her next move. "I don't believe you."

Suddenly, the conversation had turned upside down. "I'm afraid that doesn't make it untrue. In all honesty, I wish I was able to fall in love because he'd probably be exactly the kind of guy I'd want."

"May I be blunt?" Annalise asked.

Lucy forced a smile. "I thought you were being blunt."

"Well, here's more of it, then. Don't be so enchanted with your own neuroses that you turn yourself into some terribly romantic Brontë heroine. You might miss out on something very, very special. My mother loved my father for her entire life, yet she couldn't bring herself to admit that she needed him. I made the mistake of falling madly in love with a married man and I never got over him. There's nothing standing in your way, Lucy, except what's bouncing around in your head."

"Maybe that's true," Lucy said. "It probably is. But it doesn't change anything."

Annalise slowly stood. "It does if you let it." She glanced around, then checked her watch. "I have about fifteen minutes before I need to leave. Why don't you show me this cabin you built? It looked rather impressive on the hike up."

Lucy stood and walked to the door. She slipped her feet into her boots then pulled on her jacket. "I know we made an agreement that you could knock it down after I left, but it might be nice for storage."

As they walked outside, Lucy heard the distant sound of a helicopter. Annalise smiled, setting her pack at the bottom of the porch steps. "That's my ride. I have to attend a fund-raiser tonight and my sweetheart was afraid I wouldn't make it back in time. Come along, we still have a couple of minutes to see your cabin."

They walked down to the log building and Lucy opened the door. Annalise stepped inside and slowly walked around the perimeter of the room. "This is quite a project," she said. "If you can do this, then I have no doubt you can do anything you set your mind to." She smiled. "Let yourself fall in love, Lucy. At least once in your life, let it happen."

As they walked back to the porch, Lucy pondered the suggestion. Would it be such a terrible thing to allow herself just one shot at love? Eli was the most suitable candidate who'd come along. Why not try?

When they reached the porch, Annalise grabbed her pack and pulled the strap over her shoulder. "Would you like to come with me? It might be nice to spend a few nights in town. I'm sure Eli would be happy to see you."

"I can't," Lucy said. "But thank you for coming. I've enjoyed our visit."

"So have I. But you may want to keep this talk our little secret. Eli hates it when I interfere in his life."

"Our secret," Lucy said.

She watched as Annalise stepped into her snow-shoes, then started across the meadow toward the waiting helicopter. Once she was inside, the black chopper rose up in a swirl of snow then tilted and headed away from the cabin. Lucy waited until it disappeared behind a snow-covered ridge. A few moments later, a familiar quiet descended over the meadow.

Lucy had always heard mother-in-law horror stories and now she could understand exactly what they were all about.

But in the end, all that Annalise really wanted was for her son to be happy. And wasn't that what Lucy wanted for Eli, too?

8

December

ELI SAW THE EMAIL when he signed on to upload the week's video footage. The subject line was appropriately shocking. *Pulling the plug.* He opened the email from the producers and skimmed the contents, then cursed softly.

He'd known the day would probably come but it had seemed like the longer they went without hearing, the better the odds were that they'd be allowed to finish. In truth, Eli was hoping they'd at least let them go to the first of the year.

Lucy was busy working on a pinecone garland for over the front door and he watched her as she strung the cones together. She'd decided to do some holiday decorating around the cabin, hoping that it might make for interesting video. They had a whole series of things planned for December, including the search for the perfect Christmas tree.

Cursing softly, he quickly forwarded a copy of the letter to his own email account, then erased the copy from hers. For now, he'd keep the news to himself until he figured out exactly how to handle it.

He'd tried to make things better with the producers, keeping them up-to-date on what he'd filmed, letting them choose some of the activities that Lucy did around the cabin. But it hadn't mattered.

The decision to keep the email from Lucy was risky, but she was already worried and the increased pressure would only make it more difficult for her.

Strangely, Eli didn't feel guilty for the deception. He'd never lied to Lucy, never kept anything from her for very long—except for his true feelings. His only thought had been to protect her, to keep her life as happy and positive as possible. Things worked better between them when she was happy.

Maybe he was being selfish, wanting the best of her, pushing aside the negative things. But if they only had a few more days in this cabin, he wanted to remember them laughing rather than fighting.

There was still a way out of this, a chance for them to continue on with the project. He had half a million dollars in a bank account with another half million waiting for him in Ireland. Perhaps the windfall had been fate, sent at this particular time to help him keep Lucy in his life. But she continued to refuse his money.

He needed some time to work it all out, to find a way to explain both the bad news and the good news. He'd probably only get one pass at fixing things, one opportunity to lay out his plan and convince her to go along with it, so he'd have to be ready.

"How's it going?" he called.

She held up the garland and smiled. "It turned

out nice. I want to make one for over the fireplace, too. You don't think it's too early to start decorating, do you?"

"When I was in town, the stores already had Christmas stuff out."

"I wish we could have lights," she murmured. "I love lights. And they'd look so pretty on the cabin. And on a Christmas tree."

"We could fire up the generator," he suggested.

"No, that seems kind of silly."

"What kind of decorations do you usually put up at your place?"

She glanced up at him. "I don't really have a home," she said. "I sometimes rent a room. Or I house-sit. I have a few ex-coworkers that let me camp on their couch if I need to. I'm in and out of town so much that it's crazy to rent a house or an apartment."

"One of these days, you're going to have to put down some roots," he said.

"Maybe," she said with a shrug. She went back to her work and Eli set down the laptop and crossed the room to sit next to her. "We got some good footage last week. The snowshoe segment was fun."

"I wish we could have found some bear tracks or mountain lion tracks, though. Lions and tigers and bears, oh my."

"Bears are hibernating. And mountain lions are usually nocturnal."

"Bigfoot would have been nice, too. Now *that* would have been drama. Big ratings."

Lately, they'd both taken on a rather cynical view of the production company and the producers' quest for drama and conflict. It had become a source of badly needed humor and when they were bored, they developed an entire video series featuring Riley and his adventures in the wilderness.

Yesterday, the dog had seen a rabbit and chased it until he was covered with snow. The day before, he'd eaten an entire bowl of oatmeal that Eli had left on the kitchen table. They'd documented his feast with a hidden camera while Eli and Lucy watched from beneath the quilts on the bed. They'd also dressed him up and done a music video with Riley sitting in Eli's lap.

For Eli, it was a way to lift the boredom of too many hours spent in the cabin. The days were getting shorter, the weather more unpredictable, and it was becoming harder and harder to tape outdoors. Lucy could tolerate only so many craft projects before she got frustrated and began to pitch supplies in his direction.

"I was thinking that maybe we need to get away for a few days, Luce. We've been stuck inside for too long and we're both starting to go a bit crazy."

"Where would we go?"

"We could go into town."

She turned and stared at him. "We can't go into town."

"Sure we can. I know the way and you've gotten really good on the snowshoes. We can take Riley and rent a nice room at one of the resorts. You can have a shower, and eggs and bacon for breakfast, and in-room movies to watch and—"

"Stop!" she cried. "Why are you doing this? Why are you tormenting me?"

Eli blinked in surprise. "I wasn't trying to torment you. I just thought—"

"No. You know that I can't leave. I signed a contract to stay on this mountain for an entire year."

"We've stretched those guidelines pretty far. Maybe we could stretch them a little further. Besides, they owe you a few days off."

She pushed to her feet, and her gaze narrowed and fixed squarely on his. "What do you know? What have you heard?"

Eli shrugged. "I don't know anything. Why would you think that?"

"You were just on the computer," she said. "What did you read?" She strode across the room and opened the laptop, then logged in to her email account. Eli watched as she searched for evidence against him.

She wasn't going to be happy when she learned the truth. But maybe there was a way he could save this all for her, without her knowing that he was responsible. She probably wouldn't accept his direct help. She was stubborn that way. But he could always be a silent investor.

Lucy continued to scroll through the emails. He loved to watch her attack a problem, to focus all her attention on it and examine it from a million different angles. And then to formulate a plan and carry it out. She'd done it with the cabin and when she'd decided to make the very best blackberry scone she could without using real eggs. And this morning it had been a pinecone garland for the door.

Eli smiled to himself. If NASA decided they wanted to send a man to Mars, he was pretty sure

Lucy could get the job done for them if they let her try. "Are you finished?" he asked.

She slapped the lid down on the laptop and faced him. "I'm sorry. You're right. Maybe I am going a little stir-crazy. But I don't want to go to town." She stood up and rubbed her hands together. "I need to burn off some energy."

"There is one thing we could do. We could work on the interior of your cabin. It could use a floor. And after that, some cabinets and counters for the kitchen."

"Why? No one is ever going to live there. When I'm gone, just use it for storage. Or a barn. You could have a milk cow or chickens." She sighed. "I would love to go into town."

"Yeah? What would you want to do?"

"I'd eat. First a hamburger. Then ice cream. Maybe some fettuccine Alfredo and cheesecake. Then, after stuffing myself, I'd want a nice long bath in a huge tub. With bubbles. And someone to give me a pedicure." But then, she shook her head. "But I can't. Thank you for the offer."

Eli walked over to her, standing behind her, his hands gently massaging her shoulders. "What can I do for you, then?"

"You could rub lotion into my skin," she said, glancing over her shoulder at him. He took her hand and led her over to the bed, then grabbed her favorite moisturizer and sat down at her feet. She wore thick wool socks and he peeled them off.

Squeezing the lotion into his palm, he let it warm for a second in his hands and then gently began to work it into her foot. She lay back on the bed and closed her eyes, a smile on her face. "I can't imagine how I'd be handling this project if you weren't here. All alone with the snow and the cold."

"You'd have Riley."

"He's a great dog, but he's a rotten conversationalist. He has horrible breath. And he hogs the bed. You don't hog the bed."

He chuckled. "I think Riley and I got lucky," Eli said. Perhaps she needed to be reminded of all the wonderful things that had happened on the mountain. That might balance out the anger once she found out they were sending her home.

He smoothed his hands beneath the baggy flannel pants she wore, running his palms up her leg to her calf. There wasn't a day that went by that he wasn't reminded how beautiful she was. From the shapely curve of her calf to the arch of her foot. He'd learned every inch of her body, committed it to memory and knew exactly how to exact the maximum amount of pleasure from it.

Finished with her feet, he crawled over her and sat down beside her, pulling her hand into his. Her hands, with long tapered fingers and narrow palms, were even more familiar. Those hands had brought him more pleasure in the past few months than he'd experienced in his entire life.

As he smoothed the cream into her right hand, she reached up and slowly began to unbutton the flannel shirt he wore. Then she leaned forward and pressed a kiss to his naked chest.

This was how it began, slow and easy, a gentle exploration. And it would end with both of them naked, arching against each other, desperate for release. It was the same powerful experience each time, but yet it was always different.

Eli pressed her back into the pillows and captured her hands above her head. He hovered over her, his lips just barely touching hers. Lucy ran her tongue over his lower lip, then arched her hips against his, smiling when she felt the erection beneath his jeans.

Sex was the best way to battle boredom. And Eli hoped they'd never find a better one. He grabbed her hands and pulled her to her feet to stand beside the bed. His gaze fixed on hers, he reached over and pulled her sweatshirt over her head.

Smiling coyly, Lucy brushed his flannel shirt off his shoulders. They were both dressed in layers of clothes to ward off the chill inside the cabin. Piece by piece, they undressed each other, tossing the clothes on the floor. Lucy grabbed the video camera and tripod from the corner and set it down in front of her.

"What are you doing with that?" he asked.

"Just having a little fun. It seems like everyone has a sex tape. Haven't you ever been curious what all the fuss is about?"

"No. It always seems to end up on the internet," he warned.

"This is just for our own viewing pleasure," Lucy said. "We'll erase it right away, I promise. It might be fun."

"You're a very naughty girl," he said.

She turned on the camera and focused it on him. "Tell me your name," she said.

Eli shook his head. "What are we playing?"

"What's your name?" she insisted.

"Ed," he said. "My name is Ed and I'm from Pittsburgh."

"Why are you here, Ed? What are you looking for?"

Eli had never played sex games, but since they didn't have any solid plans for the evening, he might as well go along with this one. "I've been looking for a girl like you," he said.

"Like me? What do you want me to do for you, Ed? I can do lots of things." Lucy stepped out from behind the camera. "You just have to ask."

"What can I do for you?" Eli inquired, watching as she slowly circled him. He held his breath as her fingers drifted along his erection. But she didn't touch him, making the anticipation even more unbearable.

"This isn't about me, Ed. This is all about you." Lucy spied a wool scarf she'd tossed over the bedpost and grabbed it, letting it brush against his naked body. "Do you like to be tied up?"

"Lucy, are you—"

"My name's not Lucy, Ed."

"No? What is it?"

"It's whatever you want it to be. What do you want to call me?" She stepped behind him and grabbed his wrists, then knotted the scarf around them. "Hmmm? Who am I?"

"Miss Randall. My ninth grade English teacher. I had a thing for her."

Lucy smiled as she stood in front of him. Raking her fingernail down the center of his chest, she leaned into him. "I guess it's time for our lesson."

She wrapped her fingers around his shaft and

slowly stroked. Eli groaned softly. With activities like this, he mused, winter would fly by.

LUCY CURLED INTO the warmth of Eli's body, tugging her feet out from beneath Riley, who was lying across the foot of the bed. Outside, the wind had picked up again, filling the silent cabin with the hissing sound of snow on the windows.

The cabin was far from weather tight, and frigid drafts found their way inside through the tiniest cracks and crevices. The old quilts had not been enough to keep them warm, so they had added the two down sleeping bags. Even Riley, with his thick winter fur, would be beneath the covers by the time morning rolled around.

She grabbed her fleece pants and a sweatshirt and pulled them on over her naked body, then slipped from the warmth of the bed, placing her bare feet on the cold floor. She whipped on heavy wool socks to keep her feet warm and then walked over to the fireplace to rebuild the fire.

Poking at the embers, she added some kindling and gradually fed the growing flames until the wood began to pop and crack. The embers in the wood-fired kitchen stove were dead and she got that fire started and then put the teakettle on to boil.

Lucy slowly looked around the interior, a place that had become so familiar that it felt like home. From the cracked tile on the hearth to the deep scar in the wood floor in the kitchen, she knew every detail of Trudie's cabin. When she'd arrived, it had all seemed so strange and new, and now the thought of leaving made her heart ache. She'd never missed a person or a place in all her life and Lucy worried that she'd miss both before long.

She wasn't sure what time it was. It was still dark outside and dawn would probably be obscured by the snowstorm. But they'd crawled into bed early the night before just to stay warm and now she was wide awake with nothing to do.

If she didn't start to get outside more, to put in a hard day's work, she'd be fifty pounds heavier by the time the snow melted. Lucy walked to the kitchen sink and stared at the cupboards above it.

When she'd moved in to the cabin there were supplies in jars and cans and tins that had probably been there since Trudie's day. During the summer and fall, she'd been occupied with building her cabin, but now she had the chance to clean and organize.

She pulled over a chair and got up on it, then began to remove everything from the top shelves. When she ran out of space on the counter, she filled the kitchen table. The last item she removed had been tucked into a corner of the cabinet. It was a small photo album. Lucy grabbed it and pulled it out, then stepped down off the chair.

She hadn't bothered to light any of the lamps, so she sat down on the edge of the hearth and flipped through the book by the light of the fire. "'What I did on my summer vacation,'" she murmured. "'By Elijah G. Montgomery.'"

To Lucy's delight, the album was filled with photos of Eli and his grandmother, enjoying a variety of activities around the cabin. There was Eli picking blackberries and Eli watering the vegetable garden.

There was another picture of Eli holding a baby rabbit and Eli standing in a rainstorm in just his underwear.

Though his childhood had been unconventional, it was clear from the photos that he was deeply loved. She stood up and wandered over to the bed, her gaze moving between the boy in the pictures and the man in the bed. He looked so young when he slept, his hair falling over his face, his features smooth and relaxed.

How had this happened to her? She'd gone for so many years not needing another human being in her life. She'd learned to exist all on her own and be quite happy with that. But sometime over the past few months, she'd become half of a pair. She wasn't sure exactly when it had occurred, but she was sure of this—she was a better person when she was with Eli, more complete as a half than she'd ever been as a whole.

She was happier and more optimistic. Less cynical. Content.

Maybe it wasn't Eli, Lucy mused. Maybe it was living in the wilderness with nothing to do but reflect on the choices she made in her life. But how was she supposed to be sure?

Kneeling down beside the bed, she studied him, taking in each perfect feature. His face was so familiar to her, the smile that warmed her heart, the lips that warmed her blood. Would it be possible to live without him? Lucy felt as if she may have already reached the point of no return. No matter how hard she tried, she might not be able to forget him.

"Do I love you?" she whispered. There was no way she could answer that question on her own. Someone had to tell her how love was supposed to feel. There had to be a checklist or some guidelines she could follow. A test she could take.

Lucy glanced around and saw the laptop sitting on the small desk across the room. Smiling, she walked over and grabbed it, then turned it on. As she waited for the satellite link to connect, she thought about what search terms to use. "How do I know I'm in love?" she murmured, typing it into the search bar.

She noticed the email flag in the corner of the screen and clicked on it. A few seconds later, her mailbox opened and she saw a new email from Anna. Her gaze scanned to the subject line and she was shocked to see the word *SHUTDOWN* in bold capital letters.

Drawing a ragged breath, she clicked on the email and began to read. It began with an apology that the network had decided to pull the plug on the production, then thanked Lucy for all her hard work. Neither Rachel nor Anna thought there was a market for the program as a series but encouraged Lucy to try to buy the rights from the company and sell it as a special to public television or put it up on the internet.

The email kept referring back to an earlier notification from them and Lucy slowly came to suspect that Eli had already seen the email and had decided to hide it from her. It was exactly what he'd do—he was always trying to protect her. But what right did he have? This was her project, not his. She was the one who made the decisions, not him.

This was exactly what happened when a woman turned her life upside down for a man. He expected to call all the shots. But Lucy had run her own life from the time she was a teenager, and she wasn't about to change now.

This was her test, her checklist, Lucy thought to herself. In one simple example, she'd found a reason why she couldn't possibly fall in love with Eli. He wasn't special. He was like every other man she'd ever known. He expected to be in charge.

Cursing softly, she picked up the laptop and carried it over to the bed. A shake to his shoulder woke him up and Lucy stood over him, watching him rub the sleep out of his eyes. "When were you going to tell me?" she asked.

"What?" He sat up, then stretched his arms over his head and smiled at her. "What's wrong?"

"When were you going to tell me that they pulled the plug?"

He stared up at her and his smile slowly faded. "How did you find out?"

"I had to look up something on the internet and I noticed a note in my mailbox. How long were you going to keep this from me?"

"As long as I could," he replied. "You haven't been checking your mail lately and— Wait, what were you doing on the internet? Isn't that against the guidelines?"

"What guidelines? The project is over. No more guidelines. I'm done. They're sending a helicopter for me tomorrow. They expect me to be packed and ready to leave."

Eli swung his legs off the edge of the bed, dragging one of the sleeping bags along and wrapping his naked body in it. "No, you don't have to leave. We'll figure out a way to fix this, Luce. Trust me, there's no need to give up. Not yet."

"How?"

"We can buy them out. Pay back the production costs and find someone else interested in the show. We could probably offer them fifty cents on the dollar and they'd grab it."

"Where am I going to get that kind of money?"

"I have that kind of money," Eli said.

"No." She shook her head. "No. This is my project."

"It's my grandmother," he countered.

She opened her mouth to reply, then realized that he was right. Trudie belonged to him more than her. But that wasn't the point. By accepting his help, she was admitting she needed him, admitting she'd failed. And needing someone was just a trap. Sooner or later, the relationship would end and she'd be alone again and broken.

He grabbed the laptop and closed it, then set it on the bed next to him. "I'm sorry," Eli said. "I was trying to buy some time to see if I could fix this. And I didn't want you to worry."

"You didn't want me to leave," she said.

"Of course I didn't. I love you. I never want you to leave. I want you to stay with me forever."

"Don't say that," Lucy cried, covering her ears.

"Just because you don't want to hear it, doesn't mean it isn't true," he said.

Lucy crawled off the bed. "And how do you know you love me? Did you love me last week, or are you only saying that now to keep me from leaving? That's not love. That's possession. You don't want to give me up."

"Don't tell me how I feel!"

"So when did you realize it? Tell me."

He cursed softly. "Right this moment."

"That's kind of convenient, don't you think?"

"You're right. I don't want you to leave…because I can't imagine living a day without you." He paused. "But I also want you to be happy. And if you can't be happy with me, Luce, then you have to leave."

"And then you'll stop loving me," she said.

Eli shook his head. "No, I don't think that's going to happen. I'll probably love you for the rest of my life. That kind of thing is in my family DNA. There's no getting away from it."

He reached out and grabbed her hand, drawing it to his lips. "It's all right if you don't love me in return. I understand. But if you ever change your mind, you can always come back. The cabin will always be here."

Tears began to gather in Lucy's eyes and she drew a deep breath to keep them from falling. She refused to surrender to her emotions. "I'm going to LA and I'm going to talk them into finishing this project," she said. "I'm not going to give up."

"That's a great idea."

She slowly untangled her fingers from his. Lucy wanted to ask him to come with her, to help her fight this fight. But in her heart, she knew it was time to put some distance between them. When she left the mountain tomorrow, there was a chance she wouldn't be returning. And she didn't want to say goodbye without the certainty that it was going to be forever.

THE NEXT MORNING, Eli stared out at the pristine layer of snow that blanketed the meadow. It glittered in the early morning sun as if diamonds had been scattered across the surface during the night.

He'd hoped that the snowstorm would go on forever, but the weather had cleared yesterday afternoon and the helicopter would be arriving in about two hours.

Riley woofed softly and Eli caught sight of a red fox leaping through the snow at the edge of the meadow. He took a sip of his coffee, then turned and walked back inside the cabin, Riley pushing through the door ahead of him.

Lucy had spent most of the day yesterday gathering her things and cleaning the cabin. Though Eli had insisted there was no reason to clean, she did it anyway in a blatant attempt to avoid him. When it had come time for bed, she'd decided to sleep on the floor in front of the fireplace. Eli couldn't let her do that so he'd volunteered to give her the bed and he'd ended up sleeping by the fire.

"If you forget anything, I can always send it to you," he said softly as he watched her rummage through the desk drawers.

"I know," Lucy replied. She paused and looked around the cabin, then met his gaze. A blush crept up her cheeks and she glanced away, grabbing a T-shirt from the back of a chair and folding it carefully. "I appreciate what you said."

He stood beside her next to the bed. Eli wanted to touch her again, but she hadn't allowed that since the night before last. "I've said a lot of things over the past six months," Eli said.

"About how you loved me. And I want you to know that if I was capable of loving someone forever, then it would probably be you. Definitely you. But...I'm just not ready...prepared—I'm not prepared to fall in love."

"I don't think you really can prepare yourself," Eli said. "It just kind of happens and there's no going back."

"And you wouldn't want me," she continued. "I'm pretty messed up when it comes to emotional commitment. I'm...damaged."

"Why don't you let me decide what I want and what I don't want," he murmured. "You and I understand each other pretty well. And I know why you're doing this." He slipped his arms around her waist and slowly turned her toward him.

"I'm leaving because this..." She glanced around the cabin. "This is over. At least for now. I don't have any choice but to go."

"Oh, you have all the choices in the world, Lucy. You can do anything you want. I mean, anything. Most people have family obligations, friends, commitments to think about. But you have nothing tying you down. For you it should be simple."

"Love is never simple," she said.

"Yes, it is." Eli pressed his hand to Lucy's cheek. "Just tell me how you feel. Deep, deep inside, in all those dark corners where you hide your true feelings, I know you want to stay."

"I can't," she said.

"You don't have to say it out loud," Eli insisted. "I know it's there. I can see it." He leaned forward and brushed a soft kiss across her lips. "You love me."

"No," she said.

This time, Eli kissed her with a sense of purpose. He ran his fingers through the silken hair at her nape and pulled her into a long deep kiss. "Feel that?" he murmured. "The way your heart is pounding? That's what love does to you. You're breathless and dizzy and exhilarated. And you want to rip off your clothes and ravish me until there's no more doubt in your mind."

"That's lust," she said. "Not love."

He let the sleeping bag drop to the floor, revealing his naked body and the flesh-and-blood evidence of his desire. Eli knew she was close to capitulation but Lucy was also incredibly stubborn when it came to admitting her weaknesses. And to Lucy, love was a weakness that she wouldn't tolerate.

"Touch me," he said.

She shook her head. "Why are you doing this?"

"To prove a point. You can deny it all you want, Luce, but this is what you'll miss. Me and you."

Eli reached out and grabbed her hand, placing it on his chest, just over his heart. Her touch sent currents of pleasure racing through him, but he kept his focus on her. When he grabbed the hem of her sweatshirt, she sucked in a sharp breath, but didn't protest when he pulled it over her head. "Tell me to stop." He waited a moment before skimming her fleece pants down over her hips.

She stood before him, her chin tipped up defiantly, her naked body trembling. Now that they'd reached this point, the rest was up to her. Eli waited, praying that he'd read her mood right and that she was second-guessing her decision.

Her fingers trembled as she smoothed her hand over his chest, then slowly dropped it lower until her fingertips danced along the length of his rigid shaft. He groaned softly, but kept his hands at his sides.

Lucy stepped closer, stroking him gently, slowly, as her lips trailed kisses across his chest. Eli fought the urge to pull them both onto the bed and he clasped his fingers on top of his head to stop himself. It seemed as if she was seeing his body for the very first time and yet, in truth, it might be for the last.

Slowly, she trailed her hands over every inch of exposed skin and he wondered what was going through her head. She stepped behind him and splayed her fingers over his back, working her way down again to the small of his back and then to his thighs and buttocks.

He'd never experienced such a slow and deliberate seduction and he'd never restrained himself from participating. But when she pushed him back onto the bed, Eli grabbed her waist and drew her down on top of him.

Her mouth was everywhere, on his shoulder, his hip and lastly surrounding the heat of his erection. The feel of her lips and tongue drove him closer to the edge and Eli fought to keep his wits about him. If this was the final time they'd be together, he wanted it to last forever.

Eli leaned back into the pillows and closed his eyes as she sank down on top of him, burying his shaft deep inside her warmth.

He let the desire overwhelm him. He was drowning in sensation, gasping for air as she moved above him. Every nerve was sparking, as if suddenly powered with electricity, sending jolts of pleasure through his body. Lucy knew how to please him, but as he watched her, he realized that she was already lost in her own climb toward orgasm.

Her eyes were closed and her bottom lip caught between her teeth. She twisted and arched against him in an attempt to find the best way to stoke her desire. Eli held onto her hips, enjoying every shift as it sent new pleasures snaking through his body.

Why couldn't she see how good this all was? Eli wondered. They were made for each other, both in and out of bed. No other woman had ever made him feel this way and he couldn't imagine that changing in his lifetime.

Was he doomed to live without love, constantly searching for a replacement for what he'd found with Lucy, yet knowing that there would never be anything else that compared to this? Eli wanted more. For the first time in his life, he wanted love and commitment, a future of blissful happiness and comforting memories. And he wanted that future with Lucy Parker.

He clutched at her hips as she came down on him, impaling herself so deeply that Eli could barely retain control at the long, exquisite withdrawal. He felt the first surge of his release, but held back, gritting his teeth and edging himself away from the precipice.

Eli slipped his hand around her nape and pulled her down into a long, deep kiss, desperate for the taste of her on his lips. She moaned softly and then tensed. A moment later, a shudder wracked her body and she dissolved into a powerful orgasm, each spasm drawing him deeper into her warmth.

There was no reason to wait then, so Eli gave himself over to the inevitable, the sensations increased tenfold by the effort he'd made to restrain himself. Wave after wave of pleasure washed over him and when it was finally over, he pulled Lucy down beside him, their limbs still tangled together.

"Isn't that proof enough that we belong together?" he whispered.

She refused to answer him and he didn't press her further. Maybe it would take time apart for her to realize what they'd shared. So he might have to wait for Lucy. But she was worth waiting for.

He drew her close and kissed her again. Over the next hour, they made love again. But they didn't talk about the future. Instead, they lived entirely in the present, taking pleasure while it was still possible.

And when the time came for Lucy to leave, Eli didn't ask her to stay again. He already had his answer and he knew she wouldn't change her mind. So he carried her bags out to the snow-covered meadow and watched as she hopped on the helicopter and flew out of his life.

He stood for an hour in the snow, staring at the horizon where the helicopter had disappeared into the distance. Riley stayed at his side, as if the dog also understood the importance of the moment.

And when the wind picked up and the sun began to sink behind the mountains, Eli trudged back to the cabin and shut the door behind him. Lucy's absence hung over the place like a dark cloud, and he closed his eyes and thought about everything that had happened since they'd first met.

"She'll come back," he said. Riley whined softly and he smiled down at the dog. "And we'll be here when she does."

9

A DRY, DUSTY wind blew through the catering tent, the midday sun blazing hot in the sky. Lucy reached for her bottle of water and took a long drink, then plucked at the light cotton shirt she wore. Yuma, Arizona, was not the most comfortable location for a major motion picture, but for a Western, it was ideal.

She'd been working as a script supervisor with Aron Melton, an indie writer/director. Her duties included keying in script changes, photocopying those changes and delivering the pages to the cast and crew, sometimes on an hourly basis.

It wasn't a complicated job, but it took focus and attention to detail. She'd worked with Tripleton Films in the past and they'd been the first call she'd made when she'd returned to LA.

She'd hoped to convince them to invest in the Trudie Montgomery project, but they hadn't shown any interest—nor had any of the seventeen other production houses she'd approached. But Tripleton had offered her a job, a way to make a living before she figured out her next move, so she'd grabbed it. A week later she'd been working continuity on a romantic comedy filming in Seattle.

After Christmas, she'd been assigned to a film shoot in Reno, and after that, she'd headed for Yuma to do preproduction for this three-week shoot, which would keep her busy until mid-March.

She'd hoped the constant work and change of scenery would help her forget the Trudie project and the abandoned romance with Eli, but it hadn't. She'd been certain it would only take a month to put him out of her head, but with every day that passed, Lucy found herself thinking about him more and more.

She replayed long conversations with him, dwelled on their passionate encounters and she'd even found herself conjuring his image in the moments before she fell asleep in the hopes that she'd dream about him.

He'd become so deeply embedded in her life that it had been impossible to detach herself from him. Never mind that she really didn't want to let him go. Lucy closed her eyes and let her memories spin back, trying to picture him in her head.

How often had she wished for just a single photograph to remind her of what he looked like? She'd only ever videotaped him, and that footage was sitting on a computer somewhere in an office in Los Angeles.

"Miss Lucy Parker. Mind if I join you?"

She glanced up to find the star of their film, Nathan Colter, standing over the table, a lunch tray in his hands. The popular Aussie actor was dressed in his usual costume—a faded shirt, dusty jeans, cowboy boots and a vest with an old sheriff's star gleaming on his chest. A two-day stubble of beard darkened his jawline and the makeup artist had given him a weathered tan that made him look even more dangerous. He placed his white cowboy hat on the table beside him as he sat down.

He really was quite attractive, Lucy mused, an opinion shared by nearly every other female on set. And though she hadn't met him formally, she'd watched him work and considered him a decent actor, even if he seemed a bit reckless when it came to doing his own stunts. She'd even wondered if he would be her next lover, the man to make her forget all about Eli.

"Hi," she said.

"We haven't met." He held out his hand. "I'm Nathan Colter."

She smiled. "I know who you are."

"Do you mind if I join you?"

"Sure," Lucy said. "I mean, no. I don't mind."

There were always rumors about on-set affairs between leading men and leading ladies, but this location shoot didn't include any actresses, so the large cast of actors had been left to cruise the women on the production staff for companionship. From what she'd heard, Nathan had already slept with one of the makeup artists and one of the horse wranglers.

"How is the day going?" Lucy asked. "Are we still on schedule?"

"Looks like we should finish on time today."

"Good," she said.

"I was thinking if we wrap early tonight, you might want to come out with me and get some dinner. I heard about this really great barbecue place on the other side of town. Do you like barbecue?"

"You're asking me out?"

"Yeah. Is there a problem with that? I asked Jenna if you were married or involved and she said no."

"I'm not," Lucy said. And yet, the moment she said it, she knew it was a lie. She hadn't made any promises to Eli; she had no intention of seeing him again. And yet, the moment she considered another man, her feelings betrayed her.

What was this weird emotional place she was in? There wasn't really a term for it. It was something like limbo, a strange world that existed between the official end of a relationship and the moment when the last of the lust finally faded.

"Oh, sorry," he said. "Hey, if you're not into guys, I can—"

"No, no," Lucy said. "I—I'm into guys."

He grinned. "Great. So, dinner?"

This was her chance, Lucy thought. In her life before Eli, she would have gladly accepted, then indulged in a short but passionate affair before moving on. Colter was the perfect playmate—sexy and charming and temporary. He had an amazing body and she'd heard rumors that he was quite skilled in the bedroom.

She'd moved on to life after Eli. Maybe hooking up with a Hollywood cowboy could banish Eli from her mind and her heart once and for all. And yet, the idea of sharing such an intimate experience with a virtual stranger suddenly seemed wrong.

It was as if doing so might somehow tarnish the memory of what she and Eli had shared in the mountain cabin. "You know, I guess I am involved," she said.

"Yeah?"

Lucy nodded. "There's this guy and we had a thing and I thought it was over, but maybe it isn't."

"I can help you with that," Nathan offered. "I've helped a lot of women with that very same problem."

"No," Lucy replied. "I'm not sure I want it to be over."

He shrugged. "Fair enough. We could still go out for barbecue. No expectations. Just a good meal."

"Tempting," Lucy said, "but there are always expectations." She gathered up her things, then closed her laptop. "Thanks for asking. It was quite flattering. And very illuminating."

"But you didn't accept."

"I know. But it kind of cleared up some things in my head."

As she walked away, Lucy smiled to herself. She'd tried to convince herself that all it would take to get over Eli was time and distance. But she'd been wrong. These feelings she had for him had only intensified as the days passed. She wasn't free to move on. She didn't want to be with another man. The only man she wanted was Eli.

Lucy cursed softly. This was it. This was the moment when she finally realized she was in love. That was the only explanation for how she felt. He'd told her it would happen and now he'd been proven right.

Jenna McDonald hurried up and fell into step beside her. "Did I see Nathan sitting at your table in the catering tent?"

"Yeah," Lucy said. "He was eating his lunch."

"Did he ask you out?"

Lucy glanced over at her. Jenna was one of the production assistants and they'd been assigned to share a motel room for the duration of the location shoot. If there was any gossip on set, Jenna was the one who knew it all. "Yes, he did."

"He said he was going to. He asked if you were single and I told him you were. I think he really likes you."

"I turned him down," Lucy said.

"You what?"

"I'm not interested in dating him. I'm not interested in dating anyone right now. Or ever." She drew a deep breath. "I—I think I'm in love."

"With who? You've never once mentioned—"

"A guy. His name is Eli. Eli Montgomery. We spent the summer and fall together in this beautiful cabin in the Rockies."

"Why haven't you mentioned him before?"

"I've been trying to forget him. But I just realized that I don't want to forget him. I can't forget him. I'm in love with him." She ran her fingers through her hair. "They're right when they say it just hits you like a truck. Out of nowhere. What was I thinking?"

"Have you told him that you love him?" Jenna asked.

Lucy laughed. "No. But I guess I should."

"Does he love you?"

"Yes," Lucy said.

"Then what's the problem, Lucy? Call him up. Admit how you feel. Rush into his arms and live happily ever after."

"I have no idea where he is. I haven't spoken to him since I left the cabin in early December. If he's still there, there's really no way to get ahold of him. He has a satellite phone, but I erased the number."

"You're in love with a guy you haven't spoken to in—"

"Three months."

Jenna shook her head. "This isn't one of those one-sided deals is it? Unrequited love?"

"Oh, no, he loves me. He said it the day I left. I couldn't say it back to him. But now I can. I love him." Lucy laughed. "See, that wasn't so hard." She bent over at the waist. "Oh, I can't breathe. Why can't I catch my breath?"

"And you just figured this out?"

She nodded, still bent over. "This very minute. I was listening to Nathan making his pitch and I was thinking that he's exactly the kind of man I should go out with. The no-strings type. And he's so gorgeous and sexy. And I heard he was a good lover, which is always a plus. But then, when it was time to say yes, I couldn't. I didn't want to. All I wanted was Eli."

Jenna slipped her arm around Lucy's shoulders and pulled her upright. "You are in love."

"I have to find him and tell him."

"Now?"

"Soon," Lucy said. She drew a deep breath. For the first time in years, she felt in balance. As if life suddenly made sense. Why had it taken her so long to finally get to this place?

A tiny tremor of fear nagged at her mind. What if she was too late? What if Eli had already moved on? Though he said he'd wait forever, maybe some-one new and more beautiful had walked into his life and he was madly in love with her now. She drew a ragged breath.

"What's wrong?" Jenna asked.

"Nothing," Lucy replied.

No, Eli was a man of his word. He said he'd wait and Lucy had to believe that it was the truth. They were meant to be. He was the only person in the world who had ever loved her and he was the only person she wanted to love.

Suddenly, love wasn't complicated at all. To Lucy's surprise, it made everything perfectly simple.

ELI SMOOTHED HIS hand along the edge of the board, then laid it down on the crossbeams of the floor and nailed it in place. He'd been working for the past week on a floor for Lucy's cabin and was nearly finished.

He sat back on his heels and admired his work. With his newfound wealth, he'd been able to have supplies flown in and the first thing he'd ordered was enough construction supplies to keep him busy all winter long.

He'd put in another window, built cabinets for the kitchen that could now be installed. And he had plans to add a woodstove for better heat. Though there wasn't any reason to improve Lucy's cabin, he'd done it as a sort of tribute to her hard work, hoping that the fates would bring her back to the only place she could ever really call home.

He remembered the day she'd finished it, the last of the sod put on the roof, the doors and windows put in. He'd been so happy for her, grateful that the long project had finally come to an end.

"Hello! Anyone home?"

Eli stepped out of the small cabin and saw his grandfather, Buck, standing on the porch of Trudie's cabin. He carried an old wood-framed pack and his favorite .22. He was bundled against the March cold in a plaid wool coat. "Hey, there, Buck. What are you doing here?"

"Oh, I decided to take my knee out for a spin and I thought I'd hike up here and check up on you. I also brought you an overnight package that came in a few days ago. Annalise gave it to me."

Eli stepped out of the cabin and closed the door behind him. He took the envelope from Buck and examined the outside. He'd been waiting for this. After two months of negotiation, he'd finally secured the rights to Lucy's project, and at a bargain-basement price.

"Something important?" Buck asked.

"Just some unfinished business." Eli glanced up. "I was planning to hike into town on the weekend. I have to place an order for some building supplies. How's the knee?"

"It's great. Strong. I feel twenty years younger—in that one knee, anyway. Problem is I don't look twenty years younger."

Eli chuckled. "Well, you look healthy."

"Paleo diet," he said, patting his stomach. He walked over to Lucy's cabin, giving it a critical eye. "And I've been doing yoga. It's good for the joints and the class is filled with beautiful women. I'm killing two birds with one stone." He peeked in the door. "What do you have going on here? This is the most raggedy-looking cabin I've ever seen."

"This is the cabin Lucy Parker put up. She did it all on her own. Dragged these logs out of the woods on her own."

"So you're going to keep it? I thought Annalise said they'd just tear it down once they were finished."

"No. I think it will be good for storage. Maybe as a summer guesthouse."

"A guesthouse? When are you puttin' in the pool?"

Eli chuckled. "I've got some plans for improvements around here. I'm going to put in a sauna and solar array and a windmill. We'll have electricity and running water for a shower and bathtub. And I'm going to expand the main cabin out that way with a bedroom and a proper bathroom. We're going to build it all this summer."

"We?" Buck asked.

"Yeah, we. Me and Lucy."

"She's back?"

Eli drew a deep breath. "Not exactly. Not yet. But I have faith that she'll figure herself out and be back soon. When she comes, I want this place to be ready for her."

Buck grinned and gave him a pat on the shoulder. "I hope you're right. Nothing worse than a guy mooning after some girl he'll never have. I've been there and done that."

"I'll be fine," Eli reassured him.

"Have you heard from her?"

Eli shook his head. "No, but then, I don't get regular mail delivery up here, the battery on my satellite phone is dead and I don't have an internet connection—but I will once we get power."

"You know, Trudie would be pitching a fit. She was against electricity for the cabin. Thought it complicated life. Once you let it in, you didn't want to get rid of it. Couldn't talk her into a generator no matter what I said."

"I think she would have approved of the way I'm doing it," Eli said. "Solar and wind are both clean and natural sources of energy. She probably would have used both if they'd been affordable and available to her."

"You may be right," Buck replied. "Sometimes, I think you knew her better than I did. You spent all those summers up here with her. Trudie and I always seemed to be butting heads over one thing or another."

"She could be a pretty tough woman," he said. "Not a lot of room for compromise with her. But I'm sure she always loved you."

"And I never stopped loving her," Buck said. "Hopefully, your girl will be a bit more pliable."

"Hell, I prefer my women built of steel," Eli said, laughing. "Lucy's a lot like Trudie and Annalise. Steel with a soft side."

"Did you hear that your mother and Richard Baskill called it quits? Actually, Annalise decided to dump him when he asked her to do his laundry."

"She'll meet someone else," Eli said. "You never know who might wander into your life tomorrow. I never expected to fall in love with Lucy and I did. Surprised the hell out of me."

"Hell, love surprised me, too," Buck said.

"How was your hike to the cabin?" Eli asked.

"It was a pretty treacherous trail coming up. The melt we had last week made the trail icy in spots. I could use a stiff drink. Whiskey if you've got it."

They walked up the steps and Eli pulled the door open for his grandfather. As he stepped inside, Riley came trotting over from his spot next to the fireplace. "You still have her dog?"

"It wasn't her dog. They gave it to her for company and she asked if I'd keep him once she had to leave."

Buck dropped his pack and set it against the wall,

then slipped out of his jacket and draped it across the back of the chair. "You have changed. A dog. That's a big commitment."

Eli grabbed the whiskey bottle from a shelf above the stove and poured a measure into two jelly jars. "I'm going to stick around here for a while and Riley enjoys this place. Now, if I can just afford to keep him fed. Thank God I've got a million dollars." He set the whiskey in front of Buck.

"You're a lucky man to know what you want," Buck said.

"It seems like our family is cursed with unrequited love. I hope to break that curse."

"Now that you're a millionaire, your prospects will improve. I never had much to offer your grandmother. Never had a regular job, didn't come from an important family. And when we were first together, she had no intention of making me a permanent part of her life. Then, after a couple of months, she found out she was pregnant and we were tied together forever. We had a daughter, and then later a grandson. Family."

Eli could now imagine what it had been like for Buck, in love with Trudie but unable to make her love him—at least not enough to marry him.

"It must have been difficult for you," he said, sitting down across from his grandfather. "Living in a small town, having a baby out of wedlock. But you did a good job, Buck. You taught my mother to be strong and you taught me how to be a man. I hope, if I'm ever a parent, I'll be able to do half as well as you did."

Buck smiled and Eli noticed tears swimming in the corners of his eyes. He'd only seen his grandfather cry once, when they'd buried Trudie on the mountain. "What is it?"

"You're talking about a family. I never thought I'd hear that from you. I've always wanted you to be happy but it didn't seem that you were interested in finding love."

"Well, I'm optimistic about that, but not certain. I could be up here waiting for fifty years."

"Another crazy Montgomery," Buck said, laughing through his tears. He held up his whiskey glass. "To love."

"To love," Eli said, tipping his glass against Buck's. "May it last forever."

Buck poured them both another drink. Eli reached out and put his hand over his grandfather's glass. "You're not having another unless you're planning to spend the night."

"I wasn't going to walk back tonight anyway. My knee may be working just fine, but I'm still a goddamned old man. I'll be sleeping on that nice bed over there in the corner. Where are you planning on sleeping?"

In the end, his grandfather stayed for an entire week. They worked on projects around the cabin, went hunting together, got drunk a few times and talked a lot about women and love.

Though Eli had never had a father, he realized that Buck had been the best father he could have had. He was honest and clever and kind, and he wore his love on his sleeve. But Eli was determined that he would have more than Buck had with Trudie.

He would have a love that was real and a love that lasted forever.

LUCY DREW A DEEP breath of the crisp morning air and smiled. She remembered the smell, as if the scent was etched in her brain. When she'd first come to the mountain, she'd tried to figure out what it was that she smelled, but finally realized it was nothing but fresh, clean mountain air.

"How much farther is it?" she asked.

Annalise glanced over her shoulder and smiled. "Not far. About a half mile to the bottom of the meadow. You'll be able to find your way on your own from there."

"You're not going with me?" Lucy asked.

"I don't want to get in the way of your reunion," she said. "I only came with you this far because I've got a climbing trip coming up in a few weeks and I need to be able to keep up with the twenty-year-olds. This is training for me."

"I'm having trouble keeping up with you now," Lucy said.

"What a lovely thing to say!" Annalise laughed, the sound echoing through the leafless trees. "We can slow down if you'd like."

"You're sure he'll be there?" Lucy asked.

"He hasn't left the mountain for more than a few days every month. If he isn't there, just wait for him. The cabin is stocked and there's plenty of firewood. You've been alone there before."

They continued their hike, slowing occasionally to navigate over ice-covered spots in the trail. When Lucy had first arrived at the cabin, she'd been ferried in by helicopter, but this time, she wanted to walk, to get the true mountain experience.

During the four-hour hike, they'd talked about

Trudie and about the life that she'd led. But Lucy had been very careful not to bring up Eli. She didn't want to know how he felt about her now. He might be angry. After all, it had taken her four months to make her way back. And all that time without a word.

She wanted to believe that he'd welcome her with open arms and that all would be forgiven the moment they saw each other again. Annalise had said that he'd spent the entire winter on the mountain. That must mean something.

Maybe he was waiting for her, hoping that she'd return sooner rather than later. Or, maybe he was so devastated by her leaving that he couldn't stand to live among other people. There were always two ways to read a situation.

She tried to imagine the scene, what he'd say, how he'd look. Would he drag her into his arms and kiss her, or would it be a more chaste greeting? As she thought over all the possibilities, Lucy began to feel an uneasy sense of vulnerability.

Her mind flashed back to her childhood, to those days when she'd first arrived at a new foster home. Every time, she'd allowed herself to hope, to believe that finally she'd find a home where she belonged, where she'd be loved. And then, three or four months later, she'd be shuffled along to another home.

Over the years, she'd stopped hoping—until now. Lucy's heart began to pound and she found it hard to catch her breath. "Can we stop for a moment?" she called.

Annalise turned and walked back to her. "Are you all right?"

Lucy shook her head. "I'm not sure I can do this. What if he doesn't want me?"

"Then you hold your head up and move on with your life," Annalise said. "Things don't always work out."

"I spent so much time worrying about falling in love and now that I am in love, I'm worrying about what I'm going to do if I have to fall *out* of love."

"I'm afraid that's much harder to do," Annalise said. "I had to believe that Max loved me, maybe not as much as he'd loved his wife and family. But we had something. After he died, I received a check for two hundred thousand dollars from a life-insurance policy he took out for us. He'd thought about us at the end, so I know he cared."

They broke through the cover of trees and Lucy saw a familiar sight—her beautiful meadow. The snow had melted and the land was covered with a layer of dry grass that would soon turn green as the weather warmed.

"Will you be all right from here?" Annalise asked. "You have your rifle, you've got bear spray. And you have a positive attitude. Now march yourself across that meadow and get what you want."

"I'm ready," Lucy said. "Wish me luck."

Annalise gave her a hug. "Good luck."

They parted ways, Annalise heading back along the trail and Lucy starting out through the hard-packed snow. As Lucy crossed the meadow, her breath clouded in front of her face and tears swam in her eyes and froze on her cheeks.

Her whole life had come down to this moment. She'd been all alone for so long and now she was ready for something more. Yet, she couldn't guarantee that it would happen exactly the way she wanted it to.

In the distance, she could make out Trudie's cabin with its peaked roof and fieldstone chimney, with her little low-slung cabin nearby, still standing. That was a positive sign. If he'd been angry with her, he would have burned the cabin or knocked it down. But there it was, a testament to their time together.

As she approached, Lucy expected to hear Riley bark and then see him bounding toward her. But she didn't. The area around the cabin was dead silent. Lucy drew a ragged breath and shouted. "Eli!"

She waited but there was no reply. "Riley, come here, boy."

Lucy set her pack on the porch steps and wandered over to her cabin, then opened the door. She held her breath as she stepped inside, stunned at the new interior. Gone was the rough dirt floor, replaced by wood that had been sanded and varnished to a soft shine. A small kitchen dominated one corner, with a sink and a small gas stove.

Lucy smiled. He was making the place more comfortable for her. That was also a positive sign. She slipped her jacket off and tossed it over a kitchen chair, then slowly wandered around the small space. It looked so tiny, so cramped, but it felt like home and that was more important.

She walked outside and took in the view, then headed for Trudie's cabin. The interior was chilly, the fire dying on the grate. Lucy bent down and dropped another log onto the embers, then watched as it flickered and finally flamed. She sat back on her heels and held her hands out to warm her frozen fingertips.

Behind her, she heard the door open and a few seconds later Riley trotted in. When he saw her, he came bounding over and knocked her onto the floor, wriggling and licking her face. Lucy laughed, falling back onto the rough planks and trying to fend off the ecstatic dog.

A sharp whistle broke the silence and Lucy looked over to see Eli standing in the doorway of the cabin, like a mountain man, his hair windblown and tangled, his beard fully grown. He wore a thermal shirt and well-worn jeans.

Eli grinned, leaning against the door, his arms crossed over his chest. "Hello, Luce."

She drew a shaky breath and slowly got to her feet. "Hi, Eli."

"I'm surprised to see you here."

"Are you?" Lucy asked. "I thought you might be expecting me. You fixed up my cabin."

"I had a lot of time on my hands."

"Not enough time for a haircut and a shave, I see." Her lips were curled into a teasing smile. "You're looking good."

"I look like a bear."

Lucy slowly straightened. "A handsome, well-groomed bear." She grabbed the can of bear spray clipped on the front of her jacket. "Am I going to need this?"

"Are you worried I might attack?"

"That depends," she murmured.

Eli took a step toward her and her heart leaped. "Are we going to talk in circles for the rest of the day," he asked, "or are you going to tell me why you really came?"

"You were right. I was wrong. I was in love with you. I *am* in love with you." Lucy drew a ragged breath. "I'm sorry that I didn't realize it sooner."

"What made you realize it?"

"There was this cowboy and he—"

Eli held up his hand to stop her. "I really don't want to hear this."

A long silence grew between them and Lucy waited. "And—and what about you? Have your feelings changed?"

Eli shook his head. "My feelings for you will never change," he replied.

"Then, why are you standing over there?" She drew another deep breath, then rushed across the room and threw herself into his arms. The moment he yanked her into his embrace, that familiar feeling of happiness and safety washed over her. She was home.

He picked her up off her feet, his kiss deepening. Even through the beard and the shaggy hair, this was her Eli, the man she loved, the man she wanted to spend her life with.

"Do you know how long I've waited for this?" he murmured, his fingers caressing her face.

"Exactly as long as I have," Lucy replied.

"Please tell me that you're here to stay. I'm not sure I could handle you walking away again."

"This is my home," Lucy said. "At least, the only home that I've ever known. I'm not going to leave."

"I have a homecoming present for you," he said. Eli walked to the small desk in the corner and picked up an overnight envelope, then brought it to her.

"What is it?" she asked, pulling out a sheaf of papers.

"It's your Trudie project. I bought the rights. I thought we could finish it. Together."

Lucy stared down at the contracts. She waited for the anger and the indignation, but it didn't come. Instead, she was grateful that he'd cared enough to rescue her project and excited that they'd be able to finish what they'd begun—together. "I can't believe you did this," she said.

"I did have an ulterior motive," he said.

"And what was that?"

"If you didn't come back, I'd have hours of videotape of you."

"I'm much better live than on tape," Lucy said.

"Yeah, I can see that now."

He kissed her again, spinning her around until she felt light-headed.

There was no reason to be afraid anymore. She'd found a man who could be both a friend and a lover, a man she could depend upon for a lifetime. The past was in her past and it no longer affected the woman she'd become.

"I love you," Eli said.

"And I love you."

"See, that wasn't so bad."

"It took me a long time to get here, but this is where I belong."

"In my arms," Eli said. "In my life."

And as they kissed, Lucy knew that she'd made the right choice. She had her whole life ahead of her, a life spent with a man who loved and cherished her. A man who would be her family. And all that made her blissfully content.

There were happily-ever-afters after all.

Epigraph

Epilogue

Eli STARED OUT the window of the rented sedan, amazed at the lush green countryside. Everywhere he looked was a picture-postcard scene—a stone cottage with a thatched roof, a bubbling waterfall beside a country road, the ruins of an old castle keep sitting in the middle of a cow pasture.

He had a connection to this land, to Ireland. This was where his people had come from, the half of his family that he'd never really known. The Quinns.

"It's so beautiful," Lucy said. "Makes me wish I was part Irish." She smiled. "Maybe I am."

He reached over and slipped his hand around her head, pulling her into a quick kiss as they drove down the road. "Are you glad you came?"

"I'm on a free vacation, in a place I've never visited, with the man I love. It's been really tough but I am managing to enjoy myself a little bit."

"You enjoyed yourself a lot last night," he teased. "At least three, maybe four times."

"A gentleman never counts," Lucy warned.

"Who said I was a gentleman?"

"Well, put on your fancy pants, mister. You're meeting a very famous person. Don't slurp your tea, don't scarf down the biscuits and don't wipe your mouth on your sleeve," Lucy instructed.

"What would I do without you, Luce?"

"Luckily, you'll never have to know." She picked up the map and then pointed to a road sign. "Here it is. Turn here. It's just down this road."

Eli made the corner, then pulled the sedan over to the side of the road. "This is really strange for me. My entire life, I thought I knew who my family was. And now, I've got this whole new family. How am I supposed to act? Do I shake her hand? Do I hug her? What do I call her?"

"I expect she'll take the lead," Lucy said. "Don't be afraid. She's excited to meet you. And I'm excited to meet her. I love her books."

Eli pulled back onto the road and, as expected, the driveway to Aileen's country house appeared right where it was supposed to be. The gates were open and he drove in, then parked the car near the front door.

"Look at this place," Lucy said. "It's like a movie set."

She got out of the car and Eli circled around and grabbed her hand, giving it a squeeze. Together, they walked up to the front door. The door swung open and an elderly woman with a warm smile ushered them in.

"Miss Quinn is in the parlor," she said. "May I bring you tea?"

"Yes, thank you," Lucy said.

The housekeeper brought them into the room. "Mr. Elijah Montgomery and Miss Lucy Parker."

Aileen held out her hand and smiled. "How lovely

of you to come," she said. "Please sit. I've been so excited to meet you both. Ian says that you live out in the wilderness in a cabin."

"We do," Eli said.

"Tell me all about that," she said.

Over the next hour, they chatted about Eli's life both before and after he found out he was a Quinn. Though Eli enjoyed the conversation, it was exhausting trying to keep up with the curious old woman. It was as if she was gathering information for a new book, digging into details that Eli had never considered important. Lucy sat quietly and listened, adding to the conversation when she could.

But when it seemed as if Aileen was tiring, Eli was sorry that he had at first looked at the visit as an obligation. She was a fascinating woman and another one of those strong, independent women who seemed to populate his life.

The housekeeper appeared to clear the tea and handed Aileen an envelope.

"We're keeping you," Lucy said.

"Not at all. I'm keeping you." She turned to Eli. "I'm afraid I've done something that you may find presumptuous, but I'm an old woman and I'm allowed my way on these things. When I learned you were coming for a visit, I called your brothers and sister in New Zealand. They're interested in meeting you, Eli. If you're interested in meeting them."

Eli glanced back and forth between Aileen and Lucy. Meeting a distant relative was one thing, but meeting his father's other children was entirely different.

She held out the envelope to him. "These are tickets for you and Lucy. Ireland to New Zealand. You don't have to decide now. But I would urge you to meet your Quinn family, before the chance is gone."

With that, she stood and held out her hand. Eli took it and gave it a squeeze. "I wish my mother could have met you. You two are a lot alike."

"Bring her along for the next visit," Aileen said. "Now, I'll expect you for dinner tomorrow night. Ian has put together a lovely itinerary for you, all the most interesting sites in the area. And you'll meet Ian's wife and her brother tomorrow night. They're also part of your Quinn family."

They said their goodbyes and Eli and Lucy walked back to the car. Eli looked inside the envelope and pulled out a check, handing it to Lucy—the other half of his inheritance.

"Lots of zeros," she said.

"I feel like I'm in the middle of a dream," he said. Eli held out the plane tickets. "Do you want to go to New Zealand?"

"Do you?"

Eli shrugged. "I'm not sure."

Lucy took his hand. "Eli, if I had a family out there, a family that wanted to meet me, I'd be on the first plane I could get. I know what it's like to grow up without those connections, but I will never have them. But your aunt has offered you the most wonderful gift. Don't find a reason to refuse."

"Maybe you do have a family out there that you don't know about," Eli said.

"Well, after we meet yours, we'll go looking for mine. Although I don't think they'll live anywhere quite as beautiful as this."

He pulled her into his arms and gave her a fierce hug. "I'm very glad you're along with me on this ride."

"I wouldn't want to be anywhere else," Lucy said.

* * * * *

COMING NEXT MONTH FROM

HARLEQUIN®

Available April 21, 2015

#843 A SEAL'S PLEASURE
Uniformly Hot!
by Tawny Weber

Tessa Monroe is used to men falling at her feet, but Gabriel Thorne is the first one to kiss his way back up to her heart. Can this SEAL's pleasure last, or will their fling end in tears?

#844 INTRIGUE ME
It's Trading Men!
by Jo Leigh

Lisa Cassidy is a PI with a past and Daniel McCabe is the sexy doc she's investigating. But everything changes after an unexpected and sizzling one-night stand...

#845 THE HOTTEST TICKET IN TOWN
The Wrong Bed
by Kimberly Van Meter

Laci McCall needs to lie low for a while so she goes home to Kentucky. She doesn't expect to end up in bed with Kane Dalton—her first love and the man who broke her heart.

#846 OUTRAGEOUSLY YOURS
by Susanna Carr

To revamp her reputation, Claire Miller pretends to have a passionate affair with notorious bachelor Jason Strong. But when their fling becomes a steamy reality, Claire can't tell what's true and what is only fantasy.

YOU CAN FIND MORE INFORMATION ON UPCOMING HARLEQUIN® TITLES, FREE EXCERPTS AND MORE AT WWW.HARLEQUIN.COM.

HBCNM0415

REQUEST YOUR FREE BOOKS!
2 FREE NOVELS PLUS 2 FREE GIFTS!

HARLEQUIN® *Blaze*®

red-hot reads!

YES! Please send me 2 FREE Harlequin® Blaze™ novels and my 2 FREE gifts (gifts are worth about $10). After receiving them, if I don't wish to receive any more books, I can return the shipping statement marked "cancel." If I don't cancel, I will receive 4 brand-new novels every month and be billed just $4.74 per book in the U.S. or $4.96 per book in Canada. That's a savings of at least 14% off the cover price. It's quite a bargain. Shipping and handling is just 50¢ per book in the U.S. and 75¢ per book in Canada.* I understand that accepting the 2 free books and gifts places me under no obligation to buy anything. I can always return a shipment and cancel at any time. Even if I never buy another book, the two free books and gifts are mine to keep forever.

150/350 HDN F4WC

Name _____ (PLEASE PRINT) _____

Address _____ Apt. # _____

City _____ State/Prov. _____ Zip/Postal Code _____

Signature (if under 18, a parent or guardian must sign)

Mail to the **Harlequin® Reader Service:**
IN U.S.A.: P.O. Box 1867, Buffalo, NY 14240-1867
IN CANADA: P.O. Box 609, Fort Erie, Ontario L2A 5X3

Want to try two free books from another line?
Call 1-800-873-8635 or visit www.ReaderService.com.

* Terms and prices subject to change without notice. Prices do not include applicable taxes. Sales tax applicable in N.Y. Canadian residents will be charged applicable taxes. Offer not valid in Quebec. This offer is limited to one order per household. Not valid for current subscribers to Harlequin Blaze books. All orders subject to credit approval. Credit or debit balances in a customer's account(s) may be offset by any other outstanding balance owed by or to the customer. Please allow 4 to 6 weeks for delivery. Offer available while quantities last.

Your Privacy—The Harlequin® Reader Service is committed to protecting your privacy. Our Privacy Policy is available online at www.ReaderService.com or upon request from the Harlequin Reader Service.

We make a portion of our mailing list available to reputable third parties that offer products we believe may interest you. If you prefer that we not exchange your name with third parties, or if you wish to clarify or modify your communication preferences, please visit us at www.ReaderService.com/consumerschoice or write to us at Harlequin Reader Service Preference Service, P.O. Box 9062, Buffalo, NY 14269. Include your complete name and address.

HB13R2

Love the Harlequin book
you just read?

Your opinion matters.

Review this book on your favorite
book site, review site, blog or your own
social media properties and share
your opinion with other readers!

Be sure to connect with us at:
Harlequin.com/Newsletters
Facebook.com/HarlequinBooks
Twitter.com/HarlequinBooks

JUST CAN'T GET ENOUGH?

Join our social communities
and talk to us online.

You will have access to the latest
news on upcoming titles and special
promotions, but most importantly,
you can talk to other fans about your
favorite Harlequin reads.

Harlequin.com/Community

Facebook.com/HarlequinBooks

Twitter.com/HarlequinBooks

Pinterest.com/HarlequinBooks

Tessa Monroe looked at the group of men who'd just walked in.

Her heart raced and emotions spun through her, too fast to identify.

"Why is he… Are they here?" she asked her friend Livi.

"The team? You don't think Mitch would celebrate our engagement without his SEALs, do you?" Livi asked as she waved them over.

As one, the men looked their way.

But Tessa only saw one man.

Taller than the rest, his shoulders broad and tempting beneath a sport coat the same vivid black as his eyes, he managed to look perfectly elegant.

His gaze locked on her, sending a zing of desire through her body with the same intensity as it had the first time he'd looked her way months before.

Tessa Monroe, the woman who always came out on top when it came to the opposite sex, wanted to hide.

"That's so sweet of his friends to come all this way to celebrate your engagement," she said, watching Livi's fiancé stride through the crowd to greet the group.

"They're all based in Coronado now. Didn't I tell you?" Livi asked, her eyes locked on Mitch as if she could eat him up. "Romeo's the best man."

Romeo.

Tessa's smile dropped away as dread and something else curled low in her belly.

Gabriel Thorne. Aka, Romeo.

His eyes were still locked on her and Tessa could see the heat in that midnight gaze.

It was as if he could look inside her mind, deep into her soul—and see everything. All of her desires, her every need, her secret wants.

A wicked smile angled over his chiseled face, assuring her he not only saw them all, but that he was also quite sure that he could fulfill every single one. And in ways that would leave her panting, sweaty and begging for more.

There was very little Tessa didn't know about sex. She appreciated the act, reveled in the results and had long ago mastered the ins and outs of, well, in and out. She knew how to use sex, how to enjoy sex and how to avoid sex.

So if anyone had told her that she'd feel a low, needy promise of an orgasm curling tight in her belly from just a single look across a crowded room, she'd have laughed at them.

Don't miss
A SEAL'S PLEASURE by Tawny Weber,
available May 2015 wherever
Harlequin® Blaze® books and ebooks are sold.

www.Harlequin.com

HBEXP0415

THE WORLD IS BETTER WITH

Romance

Harlequin has everything from contemporary, passionate and heartwarming to suspenseful and inspirational stories.

Whatever your mood,
we have a romance just for you!